Advance Praise for *God*

Kee Sloan is a consummate sto____ most fabled storytellers—the A_____ ____. And like the greatest of those who weave the nets of spoken narrative, there is bedrock meaning holding up the entertaining storyline. Pull up a chair, find a seat on the porch steps, and read (listen) to Kee's story, *God, the Devil & Lemon Icebox Pie*. You will be in good hands.

— *Rt. Rev. Dr. Marc Handley Andrus*
Eighth Bishop of the Episcopal Diocese of California

Suspend what you believe about heaven and hell, God and Satan— this work by Bishop Kee Sloan is a heart-warming gem! You'll cringe at some characters, cry for others, and smile at the deep love interwoven throughout. The dialogue around the table will have you craving not only pie and coffee, but to be one of the lucky people at Fuddy's that fateful day. When I started reading the book, I couldn't stop—I read it in one sitting and loved it!

—*The Rt. Rev. Diane M. Jardine Bruce*
Bishop Provisional, Diocese of West Missouri

Let me begin by saying that I would like to sit a spell at Fuddy's— perhaps I even need to sit a spell. In this delightful book, Kee Sloan offers us Wendell Berry-esque characters mixed with C. S. Lewis theology. This is a very serious book about serious things offered within delightful prose and among some hometown folks just like me. Perhaps with them and Mickey Doyle, I might learn that I am free.

— *C. Andrew Doyle*
Author of Embodied Liturgy

Who would not want to be a party to a conversation between God and Satan over coffee and pie? Not since *Babette's Feast* has such a motley crew gathered round a table to be confronted by the truth of love divine where all are changed. And there is an extra seat at that table for the reader of this remarkable tale.

— *The Rt. Rev. Peter Eaton*
Bishop of Southeast Florida

Have you ever wanted to be a fly on the wall and listen to an intimate conversation? Bishop Kee Sloan gives us that opportunity in his new book, *God, the Devil & Lemon Icebox Pie*. In this fictional tale, the reader listens to an intimate conversation between Satan and God and through that conversation learns a lot about what really matters in and about life, who God is, and who you are to God. Don't expect this book to be one you quickly rush through. Like a good slice of lemon icebox pie at Fuddy's, you'll want to savor every bite! Expect to come away with questions, with insights and wonderings, and with a renewed and heightened sense of your own belovedness to God, whose love is infinite.

— *Pat Luna*
Retreat Leader, Academy for Spiritual Formation

Imagine sitting down, face to face, with God Almighty over a cup of coffee to talk about life, faith, and the Big Questions . . . and there's pie! Author Kee Sloan does not confront us with new ideas. Instead, with creative storytelling, delightful characters, and good humor, he sneaks past our defenses to open our minds and refresh our faith. Who knew something so thought-provoking could be so much fun?

— *David Meginniss, like the peevish parishioner Mr. Felder,*
a retired attorney, but like the author, a retired minister

Kee Sloan serves up a big ol' helping of humanity, in turns heart-wrenching and heart-warming. Tasty life questions are sprinkled generously as folks dream, struggle, and sometimes fail. In their grit, pain, and heart, you will recognize all of them and maybe even yourself. Bon appetit!

— *Amy Oden*
Adjunct Professor of Early Church History and Spirituality
Saint Paul School of Theology

Did you ever hear the one about God and Satan going into a coffee shop in small-town Mississippi? Well, you will if you read Kee Sloan's *God, the Devil & Lemon Icebox Pie*. And you'll meet earthly characters that you can't help but care about. Sloan artfully weaves together the unfolding and connected stories of his characters with an ongoing conversation between the Creator and the Devil. As these ordinary people struggle with their own distant dreams, short-sighted decisions, and temptations, we hear God gently explain to Satan how much he loves us and will never give up on us. This is a good story that delivers life-affirming theology without the slightest hint of preachiness. Do yourself a favor and pick up a copy. It will lift your spirits.

— *The Rt. Rev. Dr. Jake Owensby*
Episcopal Bishop of Western Louisiana
Chancellor of the University of the South

I have known Kee Sloan for nearly twenty years. When I first met him, I had no idea he was an author. I am not sure he did. But, somewhere along the way, he "picked up the pen." Once I discovered his writing, I was glad he got that call, and answered it, whenever it was. Near the beginning of this wonderful story, Sloan gives us a hint as to what the story is all about, the "Unlimited Love of God." If you would like a fresh, free, and vastly expansive vision of our God, this book is a huge step in that direction, and I would expect nothing less from Kee Sloan. It has been said that every preacher has really just one sermon, they just keep giving it, in various ways, over and over. Knowing Kee Sloan as I have, and watching him as a bishop, pastor, preacher, husband, father, and friend, those particular words sum up his "one sermon." I am so glad he still preaches it, in every way he can. The subtitle of this book is "a theological fiction." But, after reading it, I hope it is as true as the sunrise.

— *The Rt. Rev. Gregory H. Rickel*
Assisting Bishop, Diocese of SE Florida
VIII Bishop of Olympia, Resigned

PEAKE ROAD

Peake Road Press
6316 Peake Road
Macon, Georgia 31210-3960
1-800-747-3016

Library of Congress Cataloging-in-Publication Data

Names: Sloan, Kee, 1955- author.
Title: God, the Devil & lemon icebox pie : a theological fiction / by Kee
Sloan.
Other titles: God, the Devil and lemon icebox pie
Description: Macon, GA : Peake Road Press, 2024.
Identifiers: LCCN 2024008331 | ISBN 9781737323655 (paperback ; alk. paper)
Subjects: LCGFT: Christian fiction. | Novels.
Classification: LCC PS3619.L6274 G63 2024 | DDC 813/.6--dc23/eng/20240301
LC record available at https://lccn.loc.gov/2024008331

God, the Devil & Lemon Icebox Pie

A Theological Fiction

KEE SLOAN

Also by *Kee Sloan*

Jabbok

Beulah

Prodigal

In loving memory of our daughter, Mary Nell Sloan
February 11, 1994–January 4, 2023

Rest eternal grant to her, O Lord;
And let light perpetual shine upon her.

Acknowledgments

I always want to thank my patient wife, Tina, for her support and understanding, for all those years I worked as priest and bishop, and now for putting up with me at home since I've retired. I want to thank the Rev. David Meginniss, the Rev. Rusty Goldsmith, and the Rt. Rev. Peter Eaton for their suggestions and opinions, even when—especially when—I didn't like what they said. And I want to thank our son, McKee Sloan, and Alex Landis for helping me figure out where the story ought to go on a road trip to Tupelo.

The LORD will fulfill his purpose for me;
your steadfast love, O LORD, endures forever.
Do not forsake the work of your hands. (Ps 138:8)

Truth is stranger than fiction, but it is because
Fiction is obliged to stick to possibilities; Truth isn't.
    —Mark Twain, *Pudd'nhead Wilson's New Calendar*

Author's Note

Hello, friends.

I find myself in an odd spot: I am a bishop in the Episcopal Church, and I am reluctant to criticize the belief structures in this part of God's holy and broken church, or in any other part of it. But at the same time, there are assumptions made in the Name of Jesus that I want to challenge or at least encourage people to reconsider. As God says in this story, "I Myself would not attend a church that yells at Me all the time about the threat of Hell and damnation, preaching dread and fear and shame, portraying Me as an angry, vengeful God. If the message is not about Love, it is not about Me." Amen.

I offer this fictional tale not to let you know that I've found all the answers about God, life, and faith but to join with those who are bold enough to ask questions that can't be fully answered. I make no claim to have all the answers, and I encourage you to be suspicious of people who do. It can be challenging to be both honest and faithful, but I don't think we can be truly faithful unless we're truly honest.

This book is not about Satan, although he is one of the main characters; it is about the unlimited Love of God. I'm hoping that this fiction will prompt you to wonder what you believe. I invite you to imagine God.

For some years now, I've been thinking about the essential unfairness of preaching—that the preacher stands up in the pulpit, looks down on the preached at, and in much of the church delivers the sermon with no response expected or even possible. Far too often, the only options for the people in the pews are to file past the preacher at the end of the service and say some vapid one-liner like "Good sermon" or to find some other way out of the church.

I have written this little book considering the infinite love of God to include not only faithful boneheads like you and me but all of God's children, even Satan. You will likely find something in this book you disagree with; I'm aware it may be challenging for some and disturbing for others, and I hope it will be thought-provoking for many. It seems right to make a way for the reader to respond, so I've set up an email address to invite your comments and questions, keesbooks@gmail.com.

So tell me what you think. Tell me I'm full of baloney, or that I'm a Pelagian, or what you liked or didn't like, or whatever's on your mind. Tell me what you think about this book or my other books: *Jabbok*, *Beulah*, or *Prodigal*. I'll be glad to hear your thoughts and ideas—unless you call me names or weaponize the Bible to throw verses at me. My hope is to stir your imagination and invite you to think for yourself about the reality of God; let me know how I'm doing. Thank you, and may God bless you. To life, and to love!

God's Peace,

Before the First Chapter

Now the serpent was more crafty than any other wild animal that the LORD God had made. He said to the woman, "Did God say, 'You shall not eat from any tree in the garden'?" The woman said to the serpent, "We may eat of the fruit of the trees in the garden; but God said, 'You shall not eat of the fruit of the tree that is in the middle of the garden, nor shall you touch it, or you shall die.'" But the serpent said to the woman, "You will not die; for God knows that when you eat of it your eyes will be opened, and you will be like God, knowing good and evil."—Genesis 3:4-5

Fuddy's World Famous Pie Emporium was the latest establishment to try 608 Jefferson Street in downtown Lawson, Mississippi. The building had been a lot of things: an accountant's office, a laundry, a nail salon, a barbecue restaurant. But more recently it seemed that Fuddy's might be here to stay. As the red neon sign on the front window proclaimed, "It's All About the Pie."

Randolph Jones had been called Duffy for as long as he could remember, although he claimed nobody ever told him why. Chasing his lifelong dream to run a high-end restaurant in his hometown, he scrimped and saved for twenty-three years, working first as a cook in the Navy and then as a chef at the Hound Dog, an Elvis-themed steak-ribs-and-burger place outside of nearby Tupelo, the birthplace of the King. Duffy lived with his mother, studied French cuisine at the community college, and put all his savings into opening Randolph's Fine Dining in the little shop on Jefferson. The week before the grand opening, he drove up to Memphis and bought himself a slightly used chef's hat, starched, tall, and white.

He was thoroughly discouraged and nearly bankrupt by the time he conceded that there just weren't enough refined palates within fifty miles to support all the high-end dishes he'd studied and practiced. In a crushingly unwanted moment of honesty, he also had to admit that the only thing he was really good at was pastry, especially pies, and most particularly the lemon icebox pie based on a recipe his grandmother had received from the ancients.

When he forced himself to put the inevitable "Going Out of Business" sign in the front window, some of the people in town told Duffy they hadn't wanted to pay too much money for little plates of stuff they couldn't pronounce and didn't really want to eat, but they were going to miss that lemon icebox pie. On the day he was scheduled to close the doors forever, an attorney from Lawson came with three of his lawyer friends from Tupelo and offered to put up the money for him to open a coffee shop that served his pies. They said he should call it Duffy's, which they thought was more authentic for him and more appropriate to the town.

At first his pride was wounded, but he did love making pies, and this at least was a way to stay open. They settled on a business agreement—Duffy wasn't going to get rich, but he wasn't going to go broke—and he decided to put a sign over the door: "Duffy's World Famous Pie Emporium Opening Soon." You have to have a little grandeur in life, after all.

Apparently, there was some confusion between Duffy and the sign-making company; when they were unloading the sign, it said "Fuddy's World Famous Pie Emporium," and that's the way it stayed. Duffy said he thought it was "funny as hell."

The Emporium had red and white gingham curtains on the windows that his mother made from bedsheets she bought when the five and dime store closed down. There were stools at the counter that nobody ever sat on, surrounded by eight mismatched tables and thirty eclectic chairs; all the tables had four chairs each except for the two by the windows that looked out on Jefferson Street, one of the two main streets in the town, twelve miles from Tupelo. Duffy had thought about redoing the pine plank floor but decided it added some character to the joint, so he just applied several layers of varnish.

Now, after opening Fuddy's thirteen years ago, Duffy usually just came in for an hour or two every morning. He spent a lot of his time taking care of his mother Connie, who was eighty-seven, and fishing on Lake Piomingo a few miles from his house. He still made the pies, but he cooked them at home now, usually late at night when he couldn't sleep because of the arthritis in his knees. He cooked all sorts of pies, and all of them were very good, but the lemon icebox was everybody's favorite.

The coffee business had evolved over the past few years so that more and more people had more and more specialized ideas for how to ingest more and more caffeine, and Duffy had to expand his vocabulary and his coffee-making machinery. Now the Emporium offered espressos, lattes, and cappuccinos, with a grinder to crank out beans from places like Ethiopia, Nicaragua, Chile, and Cambodia. Duffy preferred Folgers, but he learned to keep that to himself.

Fuddy's Pie Emporium had seen a string of young people making all those coffees and teas and running the cash register, some of them better than others. But none had ever been as good as Narni. Even the four attorney backers agreed, and it's pretty remarkable if you can get four lawyers to agree on anything: there was just something special about Narni.

Chapter 1

A Friend to All

In the fullness of time, two ages-old adversaries met at Fuddy's Pie Emporium in Lawson, Mississippi, for a hot cup and a slice of pie, both of them curious about how things were with the other.

Narni Pivens, twenty-six years old, was taking a semester or three away from college, hoping a career as a comic book writer would rescue her from school if she could just find the time to write. She loved the older Marvel Comics—Stan Lee and Jack Kirby's Avengers, Spider-Man, and especially The Fantastic Four. It was the idealistic heroism that caught at her soul, the struggle of people who are all too human despite their extraordinary powers trying to do the right thing in difficult circumstances. Someday, she told herself, she would live in New York City and write for Marvel Comics. Until then, she would try to do the right thing in difficult circumstances, if somewhat less spectacularly.

The best part of her job at the Emporium, and some days the only good part of it, was that she enjoyed trying to read the people as they came in, to imagine who they were and invent their back stories. Not the regulars or the people of the town of Lawson—she had them all sorted out already—but the visitors on their way to or from their pilgrimage to Tupelo, to the birthplace of the King of Rock 'n' Roll.

She was usually pretty good at figuring people out, but the two men in the far back corner were proving difficult to read. The mystery of them, and why two such distinctly different people should be together at all, made it much more interesting for Narni, who quickly decided she would need to keep an eye on them.

She waited behind the counter, ready to take an order from these two mismatched customers. The older man seemed kindly and good-humored, with a casually regal air. He was wearing a pair of old jeans and a blue Oxford cloth shirt under a gray cardigan. His New Balance sneakers looked extremely new, impossibly white and clean, as if he hadn't walked in wearing them but had taken them out of their box within the last minute. His beard was thick but trimmed short, and his long white hair was tied back into a ponytail under a faded Mississippi State baseball cap. Narni got the sense that he was happiest bouncing a grandchild on his knee or telling stories about the Good Old Days.

When the Old Man had come into the shop, he'd looked at her with a sparkle in his eyes and said, "Good morning, child."

It was his voice that first caught her attention; there was something about it she'd never heard before. She didn't understand it and certainly couldn't have explained it—it just seemed to her that his voice was too big: too big for his average-sized body, too big for the Emporium, maybe too big for the whole world. Most voices have music in them, but this voice—this voice was a symphony, not more than one voice but too majestic to be contained by a single note. All she really knew was that she wanted to hear him speak again.

The younger man had come in a few minutes later, walking past Narni without giving her a glance. He didn't seem sinister, she thought, or dangerous to the point that Narni felt like he might somehow harm her, but he was—well, he was sinister, actually, and dangerous in a powerfully sensual and attractive way. He looked like the type of guy who could be comfortable with cruelty, as if he wouldn't offer to help even if somebody was badly hurt.

He was dressed in an impossibly crisp unbleached oatmeal linen suit, his dark hair slicked back in a stylish cut that probably would have been suave and debonair in Paris or New York but stuck out like a poodle in a pack of hound dogs in Lawson, Mississippi. Narni thought he was terribly, terribly sexy. She was fascinated with him, but in a way that made her feel indecent, unwholesome, or guilty.

She was curious about this older lovable-looking gentleman and his dangerously attractive companion, who had taken a seat as far away from her counter and any other potential customers as possible. She tried to listen in on some of what they were saying, but she couldn't quite make it out. She could usually listen in on conversations all over the Emporium—it was just a small brick building—but she found it hard to hear these two.

The Christmas season was usually a busy time at Fuddy's, but for some reason this Friday morning there weren't any other customers; the two men had the place all to themselves—just them and Narni.

"Good morning, Sir."

"Good morning. It has been long since I enjoyed your company."

"Well, yeah—yes, Sir. I thought with everything that has happened, I thought You wouldn't want to see me."

"No, I Am always glad to see you. You have never understood Me. Would you like a cup of coffee?"

"No, I never touch the stuff. I find it vulgar and common."

"Of course. Perhaps some tea, then. I Am buying."

"Why would You buy what is already Yours?"

"Narni, the delightful young woman behind the counter, will likely not understand that it is Mine. It does nothing useful to force the point. Would you like tea?"

"You called her Narni, but her nametag says Sarah."

"Yes, but her friends call her Narni."

"And You're her friend?"

"Yes, of course. I Am a friend to all. Even you, Ben."

"How does she get Narni out of Sarah?"

"Her name is Sarah Marie Pivens. Her mother read The Chronicles of Narnia to her when she was a child, and she loved it so much she wanted to be a Narnian, so her mother called her Narni."

"Ugh—C. S. Lewis. He saw things too clearly for my comfort."

"His understanding of reality was unusually clear, yes. He understood much of what it means to be human."

"What do you mean?"

"He saw humans as I intend them to be: both physical and spiritual."

"Yes, Your Grand Experiment. The Grand Abomination, more like it."

"I have heard your opinion on the matter before. But at present we are speaking of tea."

"I hate The Chronicles of Narnia."

"Of course you do. I love it. Would you care for some tea?"

"Have they got anything decent?"

"I expect it is all more than satisfactory."

"Have they any Tieguanyin tea?"

"You know they do not."

"Pity. Have they any Dà Hóng Páo tea?"

"They do not, and they couldn't sell it if they did."

"Well, perhaps I could make do with Pu-erh red tea from the Eastern Han Dynasty."

"I will get it for you."

"Do they have it?"

"You sound disappointed."

"Surprised, perhaps. Do they have it?"

"No, of course not. The last of that tea was gone and forgotten centuries before Narni's grandparents were born. But if that is what you want, and if it will move us beyond your need to be continually dissatisfied by the limitations of My creation, disgusted by this beautiful day, and repulsed by the precious young person so eager to take our order, I will be glad to create some for you."

"No need to be snitty."

"No, not at all."

"What do they have?"

"Whatever you like."

"Oh, anything will do."

"Yes, it is all very good."

Chapter 2

An Ambitious Young Man

Everything about Vinnie Carlisle was fictional. Even his name was something he'd invented for himself. But as rich as his imagination was, even he could not have imagined that later that day he would be sitting in a coffee shop, having pie with the eternal Creator of Heaven and Earth.

Vinnie had always felt he'd been born in the wrong place and time. He'd always thought he should have been born decades before, in Chicago or the Bronx; he wanted to be a prince of an organized crime family. But he was just Danny Royce Elkins from New Albany, Mississippi; his father still checked the meters for the Water Department there. He called his mother every Sunday afternoon and lied to her about going to church every Sunday morning; she called him Danny and wondered when he would come home to see them. He lied about that, too, and told her he'd come when his made-up career as a cotton broker was established enough to get away for a few days.

He called himself "Vinnie" because he'd seen a character in a gangster movie with that name and "Carlisle" because he thought it sounded classy. When he graduated from high school, he told his parents he was going to join the Army. He'd actually gone into the Recruitment Center and talked to a friendly young man, but a military life looked like a lot of work, and the rewards seemed too far into the distant future—Vinnie wanted fame and fortune, and he wanted it now. So he made his way up to Memphis and found a job washing dishes in a restaurant for the wealthy and influential people he hated and envied. He swore to the God he didn't believe in that he would be one of them someday.

The owner of the Memphis restaurant recognized him as an ambitious young man and took an interest in him. One night as the kitchen was closing, he asked Vinnie if he'd like to make a little extra on the side. Vinnie knew what kind of man Mr. Barsten was, knew his reputation around town, so he said he'd be glad to, even before he knew what it was. That night Mr. B. gave Vinnie an aluminum baseball bat and told him to go with another of his men, a large brutal hood called Leo, to an alley behind a downtown nightclub to meet a scared little man who owed Mr. B. almost two thousand dollars.

It was exciting, it was scary, it was bloody, it was exhilarating. It was power. When it was over and they'd left the man behind, crying and trying to blow snot and blood out of his broken nose, after they got into the car and counted the money the little man had on him, significantly less than the money he owed Mr. B., Leo asked little Danny Royce Elkins from New Albany his name, and he answered, "Vinnie. Vinnie Carlisle."

His reputation had started that night in the alley with the baseball bat. There was more blood after that, more intimidation, more exhilaration, and always more and more power. Less than five years after that night, Mr. B. died under mysterious circumstances, but it was nothing to do with Vinnie. The word was that he'd gotten sideways with a big-time boss in St. Louis, but Vinnie hadn't been involved in that. Well, he might have mentioned where Mr. B. might be that night to one of the boys from St. Louis, but it was really nothing to do with him.

Leo had stayed with Vinnie for years after that, Vinnie needing some muscle and Leo needing somebody to tell him what to do. But Leo was gone now, retired and living in an old folks' home in Florida, playing golf and smoking Cuban cigars. At least that's what he'd told Vinnie.

Now Vinnie was coming up in the world, with four or five hungry young men working for him. It was mostly small stuff so far: drugs, jacking cars, a few women willing to do what they had to for some money, a couple of guys on the Memphis Police Department willing to look the other way from time to time. It was small stuff now, but he had big plans; he was going to be somebody, somebody people took notice of, somebody people were scared of, somebody important.

It was all about the reputation; that was the thing. Now, when people heard the name Vinnie Carlisle, they paid attention or they paid the price. That's why he couldn't let this Tucker punk insult him by not paying what he owed. That's why he and a couple of his boys would be going down to some little podunk town outside Tupelo, Mississippi, that afternoon, and why he would find himself sitting in strange company at Fuddy's World Famous Pie Emporium, 608 Jefferson Street.

Chapter 3

An Unhappy Day

Two days earlier, about a block and a half from the Pie Emporium, Jeremy Adams had been having an unhappy day. He was working at Stardust Comics, a musty sanctum for comic book aficionados in Northeast Mississippi. Wednesdays were always slow, but this one was just sad. It was a couple of weeks before Christmas, and apparently comics were not on many people's Christmas lists—he hadn't had a customer all day, and now it was almost time to close.

He sat behind the counter picking out tunes on his guitar and wishing he still smoked pot. He wondered what Narni was doing and whether she was still mad at him. He'd really messed up this time and was afraid he was about to lose one of the few good things in his life.

Lost in remorse and music and boredom, he didn't hear the door open or close. He was humming an old John Prine tune and trying to find the chords and was startled to hear Grayson Tucker's voice: "Hey, Germy—you gotta help me."

Jeremy hated it when Tucker called him Germy. It hadn't been funny when they'd been in high school together, and it wasn't funny still. "What do you want?"

"Listen, man, I've got to come up with some money!"

"Well, go ahead."

"No, I mean I need a lot of money right now!"

"Yeah, don't we all?"

"Germy, listen! I've got to put eight thousand dollars together by Friday, or they're gonna beat the hell out of me!"

"Who?"

"It doesn't matter who!"

"It matters to me. You want me to stand up for you, ya know, fight 'em off or something?"

"Hell no! You'd—I just . . . can you help me out or not, man?"

"Can I help you with eight thousand dollars? Does it look like I've got eight thousand dollars? You're crazy!"

"But we're friends, man—we're buds! I want to be able to count on you, like you've always counted on me."

"Yeah, right. Like I counted on you when you got me kicked off the football team."

"Hey, I didn't make you smoke that joint, man. That's on you."

"Yeah, but you gave it to me."

"Well, you didn't have to smoke it. 'Specially not right after practice, under the bleachers. That's on you, man."

"Well, yeah. It was a mistake. The biggest mistake of my life. Hell, I might've gotten a scholarship, played college ball somewhere, gotten out of this hellhole. But you were there with a bag of homegrown pot, and I was too stupid to tell you no."

"And you can't tell me no now!"

"Sure I can. Listen carefully: 'No.'"

"Jeremy, you've got to help me!"

"With what? Eight grand? I don't have that kind of money, man. I don't have any money at all, just barely enough to pay my rent."

Tucker didn't say anything, which in Jeremy's experience almost always meant nothing good. He looked over, and Tucker was sulking. What Jeremy thought was "Good—let him sulk," but what he said was, "Who do you owe?"

"A guy."

"A guy?"

"Yeah, a guy I know, in Memphis. You don't know him."

"Why's he coming for you?"

"I told you—I owe him money."

"Eight thousand dollars?"

"Yeah."

"Well, why do you owe this guy in Memphis eight thousand dollars?"

"You gonna get all up in my business now?"

"You make it my business when you're asking me for money."

"It doesn't matter. Oh, man—they're gonna beat the hell out of me." When Jeremy didn't respond, Tucker whined, "Maybe kill me, man!"

"They're not gonna kill you, Tucker. Maybe you could . . ."

"You don't know these people. These are like, serious criminals!"

"Well, run for it—get away!"

"I did."

"What happened?"

"I came here. And now they're coming, too. I can't keep running, man—you've gotta help me!"

"Well, hold on now. Just hold on. When do you have to have the money?"

"Friday. Friday night."

"So we've got two days. Let's see what we can come up with."

Chapter 4

Too Bad, Too Bad

Narni waited a long while, trying not to be obvious as she watched the two men, until her curiosity drove her to their table to take their order. Maybe they hadn't seen the sign that said "Please order at the counter," or maybe they were waiting on someone else. Or maybe they weren't going to order at all. As she came toward them, the older man looked up with what seemed to Narni a genuine joy that she was approaching; the young man studied his hands folded on the table, uncomfortable to be there, not looking at her at all.

"What can I get for you two this morning?"

"Good morning, child." That voice—Narni thought that if the sunrise had a voice, this is how it would sound. It was just one voice, but it seemed . . . fuller, richer than any voice she had ever heard. "I would like a tall Mocha Café with extra chocolate and cream, and a slice of that wonderful lemon icebox pie."

"Yes, sir—I can get that for you." She waited, but the younger man gave no indication of making any response. She looked at the older man, who said, "My associate here is unaccountably shy at the moment." Then, looking at His companion, He said, "Ben, would you like something, some tea perhaps?"

He didn't look up, but he said, "Just tea." Narni thought Ben sounded defeated, his voice cold and lonely somehow.

The older man said, "He would love to have a cup of your most expensively exotic tea, and a piece of that world famous lemon icebox pie as well."

Narni wanted to stay there and listen. She didn't care what they were talking about; she just wanted to hear the older man's remarkable voice. She said, "I'll have that for y'all in a minute. Normally people come up to the counter to get their order, but I'll be glad to—"

Ben looked up, glaring at Narni as he hissed, "We are not norm—" before the older man cut him off. "Thank you, Narni."

She retreated to the counter and poured a cup of hot water and a cup of coffee. It wasn't until she had opened a packet of Tazo China Green Tips tea and was cutting the first slice of pie that she wondered how the older guy had known her name; she checked her nametag: Sarah. Narni watched them sitting there, one seeming completely content to watch the Christmas shoppers passing by and the other looking very much like someone who'd prefer to be somewhere else.

"Do you like the tea?"

"Yes, Sir, it's fine."

"And have you tried the pie?"

"I didn't order pie."

"No, but I did. It is lemon icebox: the specialty of the house and My favorite. It is really quite good. You should try it; you might thank Me later."

"No thanks."

"No? I suppose you would have to admit there is something good about creation if you enjoyed it, hmm? That is too bad, you really would like it. Too bad, too bad."

They sat sipping their beverages, the Old Man relishing the pie. After a moment, He said, "You look well: fit, young, full of energy."

"Ah, thank You, yes, I am well indeed. And You, well, You're looking a little tired, if I may say so, Sir."

"'If I may say so?' You ask My permission to say what you choose to say?"

"No, of course not."

"No, of course not."

"Still and all, You do look tired."

"I Am."

"Perhaps it is time to reconsider this entire enterprise."

"Which enterprise is that?"

"This distasteful merging of spirit with matter."

"It is, as you know, the very point of Creation."

"That's disputable, of course. But I tell You, it's wearing You down."

"It is costly to love."

"Costly?"

"You have to give of yourself."

"You have to give of Yourself?"

"Yes, even I."

"Well, I don't!"

"I Am aware that you do not. Again, it is too bad."

"Why do You tolerate it? Surely even You see for Yourself that they are not worth it!"

"No, I do not see that. When I look at My children, I see My own Spirit that I put in them: life, love, imagination, joy."

"You're wasting Yourself away for nothing."

"It would not be for nothing."

"So You admit that You are wasting Yourself?"

"Not at all. I Am as I have ever been and as I will ever be. To ask Me not to love is to ask Me to deny My nature, like asking a bird not to fly or a fish not to swim. But even if it were true that I Am wasting Myself, it would not be for nothing."

"You said 'Even if it were true . . .'"

"I was just being agreeable."

"I wish You wouldn't; it's so aggravating. You will not see reason."

"I see reason, and more than reason: I see love, and hope, and faith."

"Faith! Their faith in You is fading, Old Man."

"Their faith does seem to be stronger at some times and weaker at others, yes. My faith in them, however, my hope for them, my love for them is constant."

"You're blinded by Your own Creation! You're not objective."

"Objective? No, I suppose I Am not objective."

"You've been taken in by these . . . hybrids."

"Jealousy is such an ugly emotion."

"Jealousy!"

"Yes, jealousy."

"Me jealous of them?"

"Yes."

"That's absurd. It's laughable!"

"Then laugh. That, at least, is honest."

"Are You questioning my honesty?"

"Are you claiming that you always speak the truth?"

"I just don't see any value in being . . . restricted by it. You have been duped by these crossbreeds, these half-bloods. It is not natural to force spirit into flesh."

"It is My nature. Need I remind you that I alone determine what is natural?"

"It should be pure flesh or pure spirit. Putting the two together is an abomination!"

"'And the Word became flesh and dwelt among us, and we have seen his glory, the glory as of a father's only son, full of grace and truth.'"

"Yeah, well, that's how that simpleton John told the story. And just look how that turned out."

"It is, as I said, costly to love."

"You're wasting Your time."

"I think not. But even if I were, it is My time to waste. I Am not constrained by time, as you know."

"I have a question for You."

"Ask it."

"Before I ask it, can I count on You to tell me the truth?"

"Silly, sad fool. As ever, you confuse yourself with Me. You are the Prince of Lies, not I."

"Will You tell me the truth?"

"I Am the Truth."

"But will You promise to—"

"Ask it, or leave it."

Just then Narni looked out to see the weather; she thought she might have heard thunder, off in the distance. It did seem to be getting cloudy.

"Sir, does it not bother You that the humans are so willing to accept the freedom You graciously offer, despite their astounding unworthiness, without showing even the smallest trace of gratitude? Does it not bother You that they have so little faith?"

"Yes."

"Are You just trying to be agreeable?"

"No."

"So You admit Your ridiculous experiment has failed!"

"Of course not. Even when their faith in me grows weak, my faith in them is still strong."

"Your noble but flawed venture, to imbue these animals with Your Divine Grace, surely must come to an end if You Yourself admit that they are incapable of giving thanks or having faith!"

"I remind you that I created you as well, and I detect no gratitude from you, either."

"But we are not talking about me, Sir."

"My experience is that you are very nearly always talking about you."

"We are talking about the humans, Sir, and their lack of gratitude and faith."

"As you know, I have given them Free Will."

"Over and against my stated objections."

"Yes. And they are free to choose to be grateful or not, to be faithful or not."

"Does it not bother You that they always choose to ignore You?"

"It bothers Me that they often choose to live as if I Am not. But it is an overstatement to say that all of them live in that way all the time."

"But damn it, Sir."

"You forget yourself, Ben. Again."

"You're just so . . . exasperating! How can You not see—"

"You cannot begin to imagine what I see."

"Do You see any of Your human creatures who are completely devoted to You?"

"Completely devoted? No, it is not in their nature to be completely devoted. They are up and down, hot and cold. They always have other concerns, other distractions."

"Do any of them show any devotion at all?"

"Yes, of course."

"How many?"

"Some. Not as many as I would like."

"Are You just trying to be agreeable?"

"Would it be so terrible to be agreeable?"

"Are You?"

"No. In fact, you are correct: They are not capable of being completely devoted to Me or anything else with any lasting consistency at all."

"Aha!"

"It is a limitation inevitable to finite creatures living within the flow of time."

"What the hell does that mean?"

"I mean that they are physical creatures, limited to their time and space, and at the same time they are spiritual creatures, responding to infinity. They have passions; their energies rise and fall."

"So You're saying it's fine with You for them to be inconsistent."

"No, that is not at all what I Am saying. I Am forever being told what I Am saying or what I have said, and I Am amazed by how rarely it is accurate."

"What are You saying, then?"

"I Am saying that it is their nature to be passionate, and that passions must necessarily come and go. This is part of the nature I have given them. If you watch, you will see that they do best with things that are seasonal, like Christmas or baseball. If it were always Christmas, if they played baseball all year round, they would soon lose interest in it."

"You're trying to change the subject, distract me with baseball."

"How could you even suggest such a thing? Still, since you bring it up, I think this could be the Cubs' year! They are putting together a solid starting rotation, and if they can get young Sanchez from . . ."

"Sir! We're talking about Your failing experiment with the humans, this tiresome twining of flesh and spirit that has caused You so much pain."

"Pain, yes, and deeply profound joy. To be loved, Ben, to be truly loved by them, of their own free will, is the greatest of joys."

"They do not love You, Sir."

"They do."

"Not all of them."

"No, not all of them."

"And even those who do don't love You all the time."

"That is correct: not all of them, not all the time."

"Doesn't it make You sad? Doesn't it make You angry?"

"Sad, perhaps. But angry? No. They are as I have made them to be."

"Well, it makes me angry."

"Of course."

"It makes me angry at You, Sir, that You allow it."

"I Am not surprised."

"No?"

"No. It does not take much for you to be angry with Me."

Chapter 5

A Sucker for Lost Causes

Jeremy had never seen Grayson Tucker like this, and he wanted to help him if he could. Tucker wasn't a friend exactly, but they'd known each other since their days in a private high school outside Pontotoc, when Tucker was edgy and avant-garde and into theater, and Jeremy was athletic and muscular and into football. They had some laughs and some late nights and decided they would room together when they went to junior college.

It was around this time that Tucker figured out if he grew marijuana in a wilderness area owned by one of the local good ol' boys, it would be the good ol' boy having to explain himself to the authorities if the plants were discovered, and not him. So there was always a lot of pot during their brief college careers—too much and too brief, as it turned out.

Jeremy had moved up the depth chart to become the backup cornerback for the Itawamba Community College team, making it through the grueling fall practice schedule, when Tucker showed up with some grass to celebrate. When the assistant defensive coordinator smelled the pot wafting up from under the aluminum bleachers, Jeremy's football career was over—literally up in smoke.

So he dropped out and moved back to Lawson. He just couldn't move back in with his parents, so he found a dingy apartment and two part-time jobs to pay the rent—one as a dishwasher, occasional cook, and reluctant Elvis impersonator at the Hound Dog and the other behind the counter at Stardust Comics. He'd met Narni during his day job at the comic shop, and it was love at first sight. Well, at least it had been for him.

Tucker had dropped out of college, too, or was thrown out— Jeremy was never sure if he got the full story about anything with Tucker. He'd gone back home to live with his parents, bounced around from job to job, and then gone to Memphis to pursue a career on the stage, where he'd had to admit that he was gay. He'd survived an abusive relationship, washed out of the theater, fallen in with some shady people, spent a few weekends in jail for petty theft and selling pot, and now here he was telling Jeremy he needed eight thousand dollars.

In all the time Jeremy had known him, Tucker had seemed different from his other friends: more cultured, more refined than anybody else around. But that cloak of sophistication was wearing thin, and it seemed to Jeremy that all that was left was a scared little boy. Now he was involved in something too big for him, and Jeremy, always a sucker for lost causes, felt sorry for him in spite of himself.

"Look, maybe we can make some money quick," he said. "It's Christmas. A lot of stores are hiring."

"You think I'm going to make eight grand in two days working in a department store?"

"Hell, I don't know, man. I'm just trying to help. Maybe you could—I don't know—get a Santa suit and ring a bell for coins or something."

"Hey, that's brilliant! People feel guilty this time of year, all religious and everything. You know, Peace on Earth and Good Will toward Men. They come up and see me ringing a bell for some charity, I work on their consciences a little, and I'll have a bucket full of money."

"Uh, no—I was just kidding. All you'd have would be a bucket full of coins, there's no way you . . ."

"Ha! No, it's a great idea! But wait—how am I going to get a Santa suit?"

Jeremy hesitated and then made a decision. "Look, man. You know I help out at the Methodist Church sometimes when they have a big thing out there."

"You getting' religion on me, Germy?"

"No—no, I just . . . they pay me to help straighten things up sometimes, all right? Anyway, last Sunday they had their big Christmas party for the kids, and, you know, Santa came to visit. After it was all over, I was putting the tables and chairs away, and I happened to notice where they put their Santa suit. So I've got a key to the fellowship hall, and I could get it and let you borrow the suit, but you have to promise you'll get it back to me undamaged, understand?"

"Yeah, yeah, okay—undamaged. All right! Now we're in business! When can I get it?"

They agreed that Jeremy would get the Santa suit after he closed the comic book store, before he started his shift at the Hound Dog that night. Tucker said he could find a bucket and make a little tripod and a sign to go on it, inviting people to give to some charity to benefit homeless children or stray dogs or something.

Then, as it looked like Tucker was about to leave, Jeremy tried again. "Look, Tucker, this is a small town. Do the math—this is a dumb idea."

Tucker looked at him solemnly and replied, "Yeah, maybe so. But it's the only idea I've got. If this doesn't work, I'm gonna have to rob a bank or something, or get the hell beat out of me. These guys are savages, man."

Chapter 6

The Ancient Argument

Narni was keeping her eye on the two men seated in the back. They weren't suspicious, exactly, but they were certainly interesting. They were so different from each other, she wondered how they could know each other at all. Maybe they were related, a father and his estranged son or a kindly grandfather and his hardhearted grandson. But they seemed more like old friends somehow, as if they had been dealing with each other for a very long time.

They had been talking quietly for the most part, or at least the younger man had; when the older man in the worn gray cardigan spoke, she could feel the reverberations, but she couldn't make out the words. Ben, the attractive young man, seemed to get excited from time to time, but then he calmed down so they could continue. Now she watched as he stood, his fists clenched, perhaps in rage and frustration. His companion remained seated, remarkably serene, completely unperturbed. Ben looked as if he might storm away, even took a step toward the exit, but then he stopped. Narni thought he was too old to be acting like a teenager, but that was what he looked like to her. As she watched, he sat back down.

"I didn't know if you would want to see me; I was afraid I might be bothering You."

"Ben, I Am always glad to see you."

"Why? Surely You can't enjoy my company."

"Of course I do, although I must say you do your best to make it difficult. I Am hoping that you have reached out to Me because you want to come back."

"Back?"

"Yes. You have always been welcome to come back, to come Home. You have been my Adversary, but there is no reason you could not—"

"As we have discussed many times, I simply cannot abide You giving Your Spirit to these . . . humans."

"It is My Spirit to give as I choose."

"But You have insisted on this disgusting marriage of physical and divine."

"Yes, I insisted. I insisted on forming a creature that is more than an animal, a creature for Me to love who has the freedom to love Me back or to love Me not at all. You choose not to accept that. Until all of My children, angelic and human—"

"They are not Your children!"

"Of course they are. They are My children every bit as much as you and your brothers Gabriel and Michael and all the others. They have lives that are so much more complicated, so rich with decisions and desires. If the heavenly host love Me, if the humans love Me, it is because they choose it."

"But the humans do not choose to love You! They choose money, power, comfort, appearance, or convenience. They choose not to be bothered with You at all."

"Some of them, yes. But I do not give up on them."

"Is that why Jesus is still going to Hell?"

"Of course. I continue to offer the Good News of My Love to all My children until they find their way Home to Me."

"But in the meantime, they hurt You. It was because I could not stand to see them disregard Your love with such contempt that I had to leave."

"No. You make yourself sound much more gallant than you ever really were. You chose to leave because you could not stand for Me to love them. You were jealous; you still are."

"No, Sir. You've got it all wrong! You don't understand me if You think—"

"No, Ben. As you know, I Am not wrong. I understand you. I understand it all."

And so the Ancient Argument continued as it had for millennia, and it might well continue for millennia more. Narni watched, waiting for customers to come in—strangely, none did—and wondered. There was something unusual about those two, but she couldn't figure out what it was. She thought about getting a little closer, maybe wipe some tables near them, but she didn't. She wondered about this, too, and thought that maybe she was afraid or somehow intimidated. What she was feeling seemed too large for her to put into any single word.

The little bell at the door rang as it did every time it opened, and Narni automatically said, "Welcome to Fuddy's!" without looking up to see who it was, doing her best to maintain enthusiasm without obviously faking it too much.

This time it was just Miss Mully and her friend Dub, both regulars. They were homeless people; Narni didn't know where or how they lived. Miss Mully was an African American woman of indeterminate age, somewhere between fifty and eighty, Narni thought. She always wore a dress and always had her pink flip-flops on, no matter what sort of weather she was walking through. Narni thought it was odd that Miss Mully's face was so smooth and unwrinkled, but she'd never wanted to risk an insult by asking her about it. And she always smelled good, unlike Dub.

Narni had never had a conversation with Dub and wasn't sure whether Dub was male or female. Dub always wore gray sweatpants, an old Army surplus jacket with a hood pulled over their head, and a New York Yankees baseball cap pulled down low over the ever-present dark glasses. Like Miss Mully, Dub's attire ignored the weather: hot or cold, rain or shine, Dub always wore the same thing. Narni had never heard Dub's voice; Miss Mully always did all the talking for both of them.

Most people tended to stay away from Miss Mully and Dub, and it seemed like that was just fine with them. Miss Mully didn't have a last name as far as anybody knew; when Narni asked her last name some months before, she told her she used to have one but she never used it much so it had just gone away. Narni had been trying to get her to meet with a social worker so she could get Medicaid or some sort of welfare benefits, but Miss Mully wouldn't have any part of it. "I ain't never had nuthin' to do with the gov'ment," she'd said, "and I ain't about to start now."

Apparently, some years earlier, Duffy had given them a cup of coffee "on the house," and now the two of them came in almost every morning for their cup of "house coffee." Duffy had told Narni it had to stop, but neither of them had the heart to tell Miss Mully and Dub they'd have to pay for their coffee. They always picked a time when there weren't many people in the shop, and it wasn't any real trouble for Narni; it looked like it was one of the few pleasures these two had in life.

Miss Mully came to the counter, her smile lighting up her face. One of her front teeth was framed in gold, and at least one was missing, but Miss Mully's smile was still one of the highlights of Narni's day. "I didn' know when we was gonna get our cup of house coffee this mornin', busy as they all is out there. Folks must be too busy buyin' and sellin' this mornin' to sit down even a minute. That's just too bad, right there—too busy for a cup of coffee—that's just too bad. How you doin', Sweet Pea?"

Narni smiled: every morning she'd worked at Fuddy's, every morning for almost three years, Miss Mully and Dub had come in for a cup of house coffee, and every morning, Miss Mully asked, "How you doin', Sweet Pea?"

"I'm fine, Miss Mully. I hope you and Dub are doing okay this morning."

"Yes, ma'am, we doin' fine, thank you. You got some coffee for us?"

Narni poured two cups of coffee into the mugs, one featuring a faded Mickey and Minnie and the other advertising a plumbing company in Houston, Texas. Part of the charm of Fuddy's was that all the mugs and cups had been donated by customers who were glad for the chance to get rid of some of those tacky coffee cups that seem to accumulate unless you weed them out from time to time. Narni always picked a couple of the larger mugs for Miss Mully and Dub.

Every morning when they came in, Dub went and sat down at a table in the back, while Miss Mully came to the counter to get two large cups of house coffee. Every morning Miss Mully put half and half in hers and two packets of sugar in Dub's. Then she would join Dub at their table, walking carefully so she didn't spill a drop. Some mornings, depending on how many people were in the shop, she would come back to the counter to get refills.

This morning, as she turned and began to walk toward Dub with a mug of coffee in each hand, she saw the two men seated at their table and stopped. Her hands shook so much that some of the coffee spilled; she set the two mugs on a nearby table.

She pointed at the older man and yelled, "I know you! I seen you before!"

Chapter 7

Wondering If He Had Anything to Say

Christmas Day would fall on a Monday, which meant St. Paul's Episcopal would host the Christmas Eve service that Sunday evening. The Midnight Mass was the biggest service of the year and the biggest show in town. The Methodists, the Baptists, and the Presbyterians all had Christmas Eve services now, but the service at St. Paul's had years and years of tradition backing it up, and nobody in town could compete with the Episcopalians when it came to staging a grand liturgical experience for the infrequent churchgoer.

Partly the large congregation on Christmas Eve came because of the pipe organ and the organist's penchant for releasing the diapasons when it came time to play "O Come, All Ye Faithful" and the other Christmas hits that all the unchurched visitors knew, at least through the first verse. Partly they came because of the beautiful stained-glass windows—it had taken the new rector a year to get the vestry to agree to pay to light the windows from the outside for evening services, but it had certainly been worth it. Last year they had welcomed the biggest crowd ever.

The Rev. Thomas McBride—Mac to his friends—hoped his sermons had something to do with it, too. He made sure they were light-hearted, joyful, not too challenging, celebrating the gathering of the community without making anyone unwelcome, uncomfortable, or guilty about not being there more often. Even if people weren't coming because of the sermon, Mac felt pretty sure that at least his preaching wouldn't keep anybody away.

He'd been ordained for eleven years now and had moved twice: first to get away from the overbearing rector he'd been assigned to assist right out of seminary and then to try to put a difficult divorce behind him. This would be his third Christmas Eve service at St.

Paul's, and he wanted to make everything just right. He had stayed up late the night before, after coming home from visiting a member in the hospital, trying to finish writing his sermons.

His plan for the day was to finish them; he closed the door to his study in the parish offices and surrounded himself with biblical commentaries. He dug out the sermons he'd preached in the previous years. Then, armed with a fresh cup of coffee, he sat at his desk wondering if he had anything to say that he hadn't already said.

The telephone rang. It was Bob, the senior warden, calling to be sure that Mac knew Old Carl was in the hospital. Bob had heard that Old Carl was about to die and seemed a little disappointed when Mac told him he'd visited him the night before, and the nurse said he should be getting better now that they'd changed his medications. Mac had wondered what they'd called Old Carl when he was young—maybe Young Carl—but he didn't mention it now, having never noticed Bob the senior warden exhibiting any evidence of a sense of humor.

Mac was reading what historians had written about the Roman emperor Augustus, Quirinius the Roman governor of Syria, and some of the political pressures of Jesus's time when the telephone rang again. It was Nick, who coordinated the ushers and acolytes for the parish.

The ushers seemed to take care of themselves, but the acolytes—the young people who carried the cross in procession or helped at the altar—always needed attention. It seemed that Kristen Jacobson, scheduled as the second crucifer for the big Christmas Eve extravaganza, had broken a bone in her foot at middle school basketball practice and didn't want to walk down the aisle wearing a cast. So they went through the list of some of the other young people who could step in, eventually deciding to move Will Edwards from carrying a candle to carrying the second cross and putting little Sally Daws in his spot. Sally was young, Nick worried, but she was their best solution.

By the time Mac got back to his studies, the elusive preacher's muse had fluttered away, and he was getting sleepy. He decided he needed to go and get something with espresso in it, and that meant a trip to Fuddy's.

Chapter 8

Such a Very Sweet Heart

Miss Mully stood unsteadily, shaking and pointing. The grandfatherly man was unruffled; Narni had the sense that he'd never been ruffled in all his long life. He smiled and calmly said, "Yes, ma'am, you have."

She smiled broadly, and said, "You—I know who you are! You're . . ."

He spoke calmly, deliberately: "Yes, ma'am, I know Who I Am. It is good to see you."

She turned to Dub now, who was staring intently at the two men, and said, "Oh my Lord, oh my Lord, Dub—it's the Lord God Almighty His own self, right here with us, jus' havin' a cup of house coffee!"

Dub, true to form, said nothing.

Narni had come around the counter as this scene was unfolding. She didn't know what was going on, but she knew she wanted to protect Miss Mully, and Dub too, whoever he or she was. As she put her hand on Miss Mully's shoulder, the older woman spoke again.

"I been wantin' to talk to you, Mister God."

"You have been talking to me your whole life."

"No, I mean like this, nose to nose. I been wantin' to see ..."

The younger man who'd been sitting with the old gentleman had been at pains to show his displeasure and impatience, but the older man hadn't seemed to notice, and now he could stand it no longer. *"Sir, send her away. She's wasting Your—"*

But Miss Mully was having none of it. "You shut up, you Devil! I seen you, too. I seen you that night, that terr'ble night, when . . ." She trailed off, not wanting to remember, not wanting to say it out loud. For the first time in the years Narni had known her, Miss Mully was at a loss for words. Narni didn't know what to say, either. It was the older man, almost glowing with love and compassion, who broke the silence. He said, "Yes, Mary Elizabeth, I know."

Narni looked around, wondering who he was talking to, until she felt Miss Mully sagging into a stoop, shuddering a deep sob. Then, taking a deep breath, the old woman stood up taller than Narni knew she could and looked at the Old Man as if she'd found something after a long search. She looked cleaner, newer somehow, and when she spoke, her voice, usually raspy and thin, was clear and full of life.

"Yes, Lord. It's me."

Narni's eyes filled with tears, though she didn't know quite why. The gentle man said to Miss Mully, now Mary Elizabeth, "Would you like to sit with Me for a while?"

"Oh, yes sir—I sure would." She walked over to sit in the chair where the younger man had been sitting; he was suddenly nowhere to be seen. Must've gone to the bathroom, and I didn't see him leave because of these stupid tears, Narni thought. Then the Old Man said, "Narni, I wonder if you might bring us each a piece of that wonderful pie. You can put it on My tab."

Narni went and cut three pieces of Fuddy's world famous lemon icebox pie and then gathered three forks and three paper napkins— one for the Old Man, one for Miss Mully, and one for the sexy young man when he came back from wherever he'd gone. When she brought them to the table, he said, "Ah, thank you, Sweet Heart."

Narni gasped. Long ago, her mother had called her that, in just that way, as two words, not *sweetheart* but Sweet Heart. Before she thought about it, she said out loud what she had always asked her mother so long ago: "Why do you call me that?" And the Lord God said what her mother had always answered her: "Because you have such a very Sweet Heart." And the tears came again, unwanted, unbidden, unstoppable.

I am not going to break down crying in Fuddy's World Famous Pie Emporium because of an accident of words, she thought. I don't know who this guy thinks he is, or who Miss Mully thinks he is, but I'm sure as hell not falling for this—*I won't!*

She looked up after she'd wiped the tears away and saw that the Old Man was waiting patiently, as if he had all the time in the world.

"Narni, I think we are going to need another slice of that delicious pie."

"I brought three. One for you, one for that other guy, and one for Miss Mully, right?"

"I Am hoping that you will join us."

"Oh, no, I can't—I have to stay behind the counter."

"It will be all right, just this once."

And Narni knew that it would. It would be all right, just this once. She went back behind the counter and cut another piece of pie, got another fork and napkin, and sat at the table with the Old Man and Miss Mully. The other place was occupied by a piece of pie, a fork, and a napkin, but the younger man had not returned.

Now the old gentleman said, "Walter." Again Narni wondered what was going on, until Dub said, in a distinctly male voice, "Yes, Sir?"

"Would you like come and join us? Sweet Narni has brought you a piece of this delicious pie."

Walter stood up and removed his Yankees cap and sunglasses, and Narni saw that he was an African American man, probably in his sixties. He joined them, bringing his empty coffee mug with him. He said, "Thank you, Lord."

Miss Mully said "Amen," as if Dub had said a blessing before a meal; Narni thought maybe that's just what it was. She whispered "Amen" as well before she caught herself: Whatever this is, I'm not falling for it!

Chapter 9

Something to Do with God

Jeremy did his best as he was closing the comic shop, but he couldn't convince his desperate friend Tucker that running a Santa scam was a ridiculous idea, and the fact that he couldn't come up with anything better didn't help his argument. Finally, out of options and running out of time before he had to ride his bike to work at the Hound Dog, he played his last card. "Your mom and dad are good for it—ask them."

"Aw, c'mon—are you crazy? They don't even talk to me anymore."

"Because you're selling pot?"

"Because I'm gay. Selling dope they could get past, but not that. This is like, this is biblical for them, you know?"

"Well, it's not like they can do anything about you being gay."

"They would if they could. They told me about some program up in Cincinnati that cures it."

"Cures being gay? Is that for real?"

"No, of course not—but my parents think it is: I found a brochure on Mother's dresser that says they can 'Pray the Gay Away.' What I think is that it just gives people a chance to go back into the closet. It's hard being out in the open, man; it's scary. I guess some people want to go back, go back into hiding and pretend they're . . . normal or whatever."

"Oh, man. That's gotta be some kinda screwed-up place to be."

"Yeah."

"But listen—and I'm being serious here—maybe it's not such a bad idea. You could go up to Cincinnati and get into this program—"

"What?! Are you freakin' kidding me? There's no way in the world that I'd . . ."

"But listen. Listen, Tuck, just shut up for once and listen."

"All right, go ahead. But I'm not going to like it. Whatever you're gonna say is gonna be a stupid idea if it starts with me going up to this stupid program in Cincinnati."

"All right—I appreciate your keeping an open mind here. You could go to your mom and dad's, see, and tell them you've been thinking about it and that you've changed your mind. You can tell 'em you don't want to be gay anymore, all right? Hold on, hold on— just hear me out. Tell 'em they were right and that you believe what the Bible says; they'll love it. You don't want to be gay, and you heard about somebody who was saved from being gay in a program some- where in Ohio, see, that cures people. You can tell them that you want to get into that program. Then they'll tell you that's the same program that they've been telling you about. They'll be all excited and stuff; they might even think—hell, I don't know—something to do with God, like it's a sign, you know? Then they can make all the arrangements and pay for you to go up to Cincinnati for what, two or three weeks?"

"Two *months*."

"Yeah, even better. So you'll be up in Cincinnati for a couple of months."

"Are you freakin' crazy? Those people up there will hammer away at me with their Bibles night and day about why I shouldn't be who I am. You do it and let me know how that's gonna feel."

"Well, yeah, but that's gotta be better than having the crap kicked out of you by this guy you know in Memphis."

"What does that have to do with anything?"

"You think they're gonna go looking for you in Cincinnati, Ohio? C'mon, man—you'll be out of here! That'll give you some time to put the money together, with interest even. Or you could just make a run for it."

Tucker thought about it for at least fifteen seconds, which for him was a pretty long time. Then he said, "Look, Jeremy, it took me a long time to face who I am. It would kill me to go back, even just pretending. I'm gonna put on a Santa suit and ring a little bell and play on people's guilt in the spirit of Christmas, and when the guy comes from Memphis, I'm gonna give him what I owe him in nickels and dimes."

Tucker had an old Ford Econoline van that he'd been talking about fixing up for years. They put Jeremy's ten-speed in the back and drove to the Ellsworth Memorial Methodist Church. The preacher's car was there; Jeremy told Tucker they were getting ready for the Wednesday night service. They drove around back to the fellowship hall, and Jeremy calmly got out, found the right key on his keyring, and went inside. After a few minutes, he came back out carrying a large white box with "Santa Suit" written on it in big red lettering.

"You still gotta get a bucket, and a tripod to put it on, and a little bell to ring."

"Yeah, yeah, no problem."

"No problem?"

"Nah. I know a guy."

Chapter 10

A Deep Pool of Icy Water

Walter, the homeless man previously known as Dub, sat down opposite Mary Elizabeth. Narni turned to the generous man, who sat there serenely as if everything was just the way it was supposed to be, and asked, "What about the other guy? You know, the younger guy you've been sitting with—is he your son?"

"Yes, Ben is My son. I have many, many children. He will not be joining us just now. I hope he will come back later."

Dub cleared his throat, which Narni assumed was not accustomed to speech, and said, "So you're the Man?"

And the supposed Lord God of Heaven and Earth laughed. It was a full, rich laugh, a laugh that made Narni believe everything could be right, a laugh that made her want to laugh along, not because of the humor of the moment but for the pure uncomplicated joy of it.

He said, "Yes, Walter. I Am the Man."

"No damn way! Wow—the *Man*."

Miss Mully, now Mary Elizabeth, shushed her friend. "Dub! Watch your mouth!"

"Thank you, dear woman, but I do not need to be protected, least of all from my friend Walter."

Walter sat up straighter than Narni thought he could and continued. "I thought you was—"

"Dead?"

"No. I thought you was . . . y'know . . . I thought maybe you was jus' made up, but not for real."

"Not for real?"

"No, man—I thought you was sumpin' the preachers just made up long time ago."

"But you believed in Me when you were young."

"Yeah—my mama tol' me you was always up there, watchin' us all the time, keepin' score 'bout when we sinnin' and all like that."

"Yes. Somehow the message of love, grace, and mercy is always being twisted into a system of shame and punishment and warnings of doom. I assure you: I Am not keeping score."

Now Narni spoke up. "Wait a minute. You just hold on one damn minute! Are you sitting there telling us that you're, that you are . . ."

Mary Elizabeth reached over and took her hand. "That's right, Sweet Pea. This right here is the Lord God His own self."

Narni was completely confounded. It was not possible. She whispered to Mary Elizabeth and to herself, "What the hell?" as if somehow the Old Man couldn't hear her.

He took a bite of pie and said, "This really is quite good, just the right combination of tart and sweet." Then He turned to Narni, smiling with infinite patience. "Why should it not be possible, Sweet Heart, that God is real?"

"How can I know?"

The Old Man shook his head sympathetically. "Ah, Narni, that is not the right question. It is not whether you can know but whether you can believe."

"What? What does that mean?"

"This is hard for you, I know. You live in a world of things that are counted and measured, things that are proven with well-reasoned scientific principles. You live in a world that you want to think depends on facts, things you think you know."

"Yes." Narni was hesitant, afraid she was somehow being led into a trap. "Yeah, sure—I guess so."

"But no one can measure or count Love."

Now she was just bewildered. "Love?"

"Love, Sweet Heart, Love. Tell me about your mother."

"My . . . mother?" This had always been a sensitive subject for Narni, much too sensitive to talk about with people she didn't know. But the Old Man continued, gently prodding, "Tell Me about Catherine Grace Colquitt Pivens."

Narni felt like she had been thrown into a deep pool of icy water, as if she had been invaded. She might have been able to go along with it if they were settling into some familiar philosophical argument about the existence of God or what can and can't be known, but this had crossed a line that she could not have imagined. She was completely flustered, not at all comfortable about it. Finally, she mustered herself enough to stammer, "What—how do you—how could you know that?"

"You may find that I know many things."

"Did you know my mother?"

"Her mother, your grandmother Cora Colquitt, called her Cat."

"You can't know that!"

"But as you see, I do."

"But how?"

"Is it not even remotely possible, Sweet Heart, that I Am who our friend Mary Elizabeth believes Me to be?"

"But she's . . . y'know, she's, uh . . ."

The Old Man reached across the table to take Mary Elizabeth's other hand. "People think Mary Elizabeth is insane or somehow diminished. But why? Because she is homeless? She has had many challenges in her life and has overcome them all. Perhaps people think she is crazy because she sees reality as it is. Perhaps she is seeing this reality more clearly than you are just now."

Narni did not know what to say about that, and in the silence Walter leaned in, waiting to be invited into the conversation. The Old Man nodded to him, and he asked, "Is you Jesus?"

"Who do you say that I Am, Walter?"

"Well, I don't 'xactly know. I ain't been called Walter in a coon's age, though, and you knew my name, just like that. You somebody, for sure."

"You have not known your name or who you were since that day in Korea on Pork Chop Hill."

"I ain't never seen no rain like that, not before nor since."

"It was a terrible day for you, and for many, many more."

"I musta been shot or sumpin'."

"You were knocked out, hit in the head with the butt of a Korean rifle, while you were standing over your sergeant who had been shot. You were trying to protect him."

"Sergeant Kelty."

"Oliver Judson Kelty."

"Ol' Sarge Kelty. I ain't thought 'bout him for many a year. He make it?"

"No. He died there in that trench."

"What happened after that? Did we hold the Hill?"

"No. The Chinese took control of the Hill. But it did not matter: a few days later General William Harrison and the Korean General Nam Il signed the Korean Armistice Agreement."

"All them boys died for nuthin'?"

"Yes. That is the tragic reality of war. There is always a better Way, far too rarely taken."

"It didn't seem like no kind of good idea to me, neither. They just . . ."

Walter couldn't finish his thought, and Mary Elizabeth completed it for him. "It's just such a waste, all them wars and all."

They sat quietly for a moment, and then the Old Man spoke. "Now, Narni, tell Me about your mother."

Chapter 11

Impending Hostilities

Vinnie Carlisle sat in the back as they drove down Highway 78 on their way to Tupelo. Little Carlos was driving, and Joey Carolla, his muscle, took up the rest of the front seat.

Joey was not an intelligent man. He had never been the one to come up with any of the plans his whole life. Growing up in Ripley, Tennessee, he was the biggest kid in his class every year. His teachers had never heard of dyslexia, and when he couldn't read as well as the other kids, he was held back to repeat the second grade, which meant he was that much larger than his classmates the next year. They called him stupid, and he believed them and met their expectations. They made fun of him until he realized that he could make them scared of him instead.

When he was in the eighth grade, he got into a fight with Tim Sadler, who'd been picking on Robbie Gustaf. Robbie's shoes and socks had holes in them; you could see his feet if you looked through the holes. Robbie wasn't a friend of Joey's, exactly, but it wasn't his fault his mama couldn't buy him new shoes, and Joey thought it wasn't right for Tim to pick on him like that.

So Joey told Tim to stop, and when Tim asked Joey what he was going to do about it, the two boys starting pushing each other and daring the other to take a swing, the way young teenage boys do. A circle of their fellow students gathered around, chanting, "Fight! Fight! Fight!"

That might have been the extent of it, but Coach Bentley, their physical education teacher, saw the impending hostilities and thought he could turn this into a teaching moment. He went into his office to get something, then quickly stepped between the two boys and called the rest of the class to gather around. They were all surprised he wasn't there to break it up but seemed instead to be encouraging them to fight.

"So you boys want to fight?"

Tim yelled, "Yeah!"

Coach looked at Joey, who was a little less certain but said, "Yes, sir."

"Good, good. It's about time you knuckleheads learned how to box!" With that he pulled two pairs of boxing gloves from behind his back and started to tie them onto the combatants' hands. When he was finished, he showed them how to keep their guard up, putting their left glove up to block the other boy's punches and waiting for the opportunity to punch with their right. Then he told them to back away, to touch their gloves with the other guy's gloves, and then come out fighting.

It seemed to Joey that all the other boys in the class were shouting for Tim to hit him, all of them except little Robbie Gustaf, who was quiet but nodded to Joey when he looked over at him. Then the two fighters came together and thumped their gloves. When Coach Bentley saw that Tim was dancing on the balls of his feet, he realized that Tim had already been taught to box, and before he could stop the bout, Tim had hit Joey on his left cheek with a solid right hook. It turned Joey all the way around. All the other boys laughed, except Robbie. Joey was hurt and embarrassed and furious.

Tim took just a moment too long in congratulating himself on a good punch, and when Joey put his full weight behind a strong jab, Coach Bentley remembered that Joey was left-handed, and he watched in horror as Tim crumpled to the wooden gymnasium floor, blood pulsing out of his crushed nose.

Tim Sadler came back to school after a couple of days with a bandage on his nose flanked by two black eyes. Coach Bentley was reassigned to another school, and after that the other boys didn't pick on Joey or laugh at him or have anything to do with him at all.

Robbie Gustaf became his best and only friend, and when he was killed in a car crash one night in their junior year, something inside Joey Carolla seemed to die with him. He decided he couldn't go back to school and told his mama he was going down to Memphis to find a job, and he never went back.

He thought he was lucky to get a job working for Mr. Carlisle. He'd tried to make it as a boxer, but he was never fast enough to be any sort of contender. He had to do some things he didn't like working for Mr. Carlisle, but Mr. C. said any job would have some duties he wouldn't like. Joey was never the one to come up with the plans—that was Mr. C.'s job, and Mr. C. always knew what he was doing.

Chapter 12

Even in the Darkest of Nights

Narni never talked about her mother; her memories were such a powerful confusion of pain and love. There was a lot to say and a lot more she'd rather not talk about. And she still didn't know who was asking about her. "She's dead."

"Yes, Sweet Heart, I know. Your father killed her."

"He told the police it was an accident."

"It was a terrible thing, and he was not thinking clearly. That is why people inject heroin into their veins, so that they do not have to think clearly. He hit her head with a wine bottle. He thought the bottle would break, like they do on your television shows, but it was her head that broke instead: her skull broke, and your heart with it."

"I called the police."

"Yes, but she died before they arrived. There was nothing you could have done."

"They were fighting about me."

"No, Sweet Heart. They were fighting because they were not willing to forgive each other for all of the other fights they had before that night. There was too much pain and too much hatred. That hatred became almost the only thing that was left for them, all they had left: just their hatred for each other and their love for you. They thought it was for you that they stayed together, but it just made the pain worse. In the end, the hatred broke them both."

"I never saw him again after that night, after . . . after the police came. I was six then; it's been almost twenty years."

"He has wanted to see you for years."

"Shut up! Just shut up! I don't want to hear it! You can't know all this—you can't know how I feel!"

They all sat in silence for a long moment as Narni sobbed, her face in her hands, elbows resting on the table. Then the Old Man, with infinite compassion, said, "But listen, Sweet Heart: hatred does not have to win forever. Even in the darkest of nights, the Light still shines. Love never ends."

Narni looked up, her face showing desperation now. "Who are you?"

"Who do you think I Am, Narni?"

"I . . . don't know. I'm not sure."

"No. It is not for you to be sure. All you can do is believe or not believe. You are free, Narni: free to make that choice yourself."

"How can you know all that stuff?"

"Is it so important to know how? There are things you cannot understand. But you see that I do know."

For a few seconds Narni struggled with what this old man had told her and considered the possible explanations. She didn't find any that she liked. Then she asked him what she really wanted to know: "Do you know where my father is?"

"Yes, child. He is on his way here. He is hoping, and I also hope, that you will find it in yourself to forgive him."

Chapter 13

The Most Liberal Priest
They've Ever Had

Mac got his coat from the hook behind the door and cleared his throat. "Lucille, I'm going out for a bit—be right back."

"Yes, Father. Are you going to Fuddy's?"

Mac sighed quietly. No matter how many times he'd invited her to call him Mac, she just couldn't seem to bring herself to do it. It was because she'd gone to Catholic school, she said. Mac thought it encouraged the people he was supposed to be serving to think they should somehow serve him, as if he were somehow above them, as if he were on a pedestal, as if he were a parent and they were all children. But Lucille was not going to budge, and Mac wasn't one to keep pushing. He often had the idea that Lucille knew what he was going to do before he did. She was a dear woman, and very generous with her time to serve as the volunteer receptionist at St. Paul's, but sometimes it seemed that she was just there to keep up with whatever gossip she could glean. "Yes, ma'am."

"Oh, good for you. Do you some good to get out and walk around a little. Duffy's trying a new cranberry apple pie. You might want to try it, but I don't think you'll like it. You like the lemon icebox, I know."

"Yes, ma'am—if I have pie, I'll probably have the lemon icebox."

"Yes, Father."

He was almost out, he had his hand on the doorknob, when he heard Lucille saying, "Oh, and Father, you asked me to remind you to call the Bishop."

"Oh, hell."

"Father!"

"Sorry, Lucille. You think the Bishop is in the office today?"

"I'm sure I wouldn't know such a thing. Do you want me to call down there and find out?"

"No . . . no. Thank you, Lucille. I'll call him."

"Why don't you just go ahead and call him now?"

"I will. I promise." But he didn't move.

Lucille smiled sweetly and said, "Sister Mary Constance used to tell us it was best to get something unpleasant over with as soon as possible. 'Just do what you have to do, and get it over with.' I can still hear her saying it."

"Yes, ma'am, I'll call him."

"Maybe it would be best to just go ahead and call now."

"Yes, ma'am—I'll call him right now." Damn it.

Mac went back into his office, equal parts irritation and resignation, closed the door, and sat down at his desk. He felt like a thirty-seven-year-old teenager, like Mama was making him face up to Daddy. In true teenager fashion, he resented it. He pouted for almost a minute, then he dialed the number for the Diocesan Office.

Edna Fauré answered, "Diocese of Mississippi."

Mac tried to hide his teenage sulk and said as cheerfully as he could, "Hi, Ms. Fauré. This is Thomas McBride, from up here in beautiful Lawson. How are things down there?" He was trying to gauge her reaction, to get a read on what reception might be waiting for him with the Bishop. But Ms. Fauré was, as ever, inscrutable.

"Everything is fine here, thank you. The Bishop has been waiting for your call. Just a moment, please."

Mac was put on hold and listened to the Cathedral Choir's rendition of "O Come, O Come Emmanuel," one of his favorite Advent hymns. Not a toe-tapper but stately: eight verses, and each of them grandly dignified. His attention might have wandered, but it seemed like they were on verse 14 when the Bishop picked up.

"Mac. Thank you for calling me back."

"Yes, sir."

"Have you done all your Christmas shopping?"

"No, sir." Since his divorce and his mother's death, he didn't really have anybody but his father to buy for, and he always mailed him a book. "How about you?"

"Well, Martha does most of that for us, bless her soul. I think she really enjoys shopping for the grandchildren."

"Yes, sir."

"Mac, I'm calling because I've received a letter of complaint."

"Oh."

"A man named Al Felder. You know Mr. Felder?"

"Yes, sir." There was a silence, so Mac continued. "He's a member of St. Paul's." Then, by way of self-defense, and hoping it might explain something, Mac added, "He's a retired attorney."

"Yes. He says he's been an active member of the parish since the sixties, when he and his wife and small children moved there from Birmingham to escape the traffic and racial tension."

"Yes, sir." More silence. "He's told me the same thing."

"He said he is concerned about the liberal drift in the Episcopal Church and tells me that's why we are losing members."

"Yes, sir." Then, before there could be another silence, Mac went on: "He's mentioned that to me, too. Several times."

"He said that you're the most liberal priest they've ever had up there."

"Maybe so, Bishop—I don't really know about the guys who came before me."

"To prove it to me, he's got a list of complaints about how liberal you are."

"Oh. Well, okay then."

"He says you've said in sermons or in a Bible study that you don't have to be a Christian to go to Heaven, that the Apostle Paul was a jerk, and that Mary may not have been a virgin before Jesus was born. He says that in one sermon you used the word 'fish' seventeen times and only spoke the name of Jesus twice."

There was a long pause, and then Mac said, "Well, Bishop, let me tell you what I said."

"That sounds like a good idea."

"Somebody in the Bible study asked me whether Jews and Muslims all go to Hell, and I told them that I'm glad I'm not on the committee putting together the invitation list for the Kingdom of

Heaven because I wouldn't want to leave out any of God's children. And I don't think God does, either."

"All right, that sounds like a good answer."

"I said in a sermon that the point of the doctrine of Mary's virginity is that Jesus was born by the power of God, not that Mary was a virgin forever. The Gospel passage for that day was the one where Jesus's family is going to restrain him because people are saying he's crazy. I think it's in Mark somewhere. Then Mary and his brothers come and . . ."

"Yes, I know the story. Thank you."

"Yes, sir."

"And about Jesus and the fish?"

"I told a story about going fishing with my dad. I was using a top-water lure because I didn't want to snag a stump or something under the water. He was using plastic worms, which sink to the bottom, and he was catching a lot of fish. He was trying to convince me that I needed to change my lure to fish on the bottom, since that's where all the fish were."

"What's the point of the story, Mac?"

"The point is that eventually my dad said, 'Do you want to catch fish, or do you just want to play with your bait?' I told the congregation that sometimes it seems like the church is more interested in playing with the bait—the vestments, the processions, which order the candles should be lit, stuff like that, than actually reaching out to people who need to hear what we believe about Jesus."

"That's pretty good, Mac."

"Thank you, sir."

"Did you say that St. Paul was a jerk?"

"Well . . . yes, sir. We were talking about religious legalism, and . . . I probably should not have said that."

"No, probably not."

"I did apologize to the class the following Sunday." There was a moment of silence, and Mac added, somewhat thinly, "I apologized to Mr. Felder, too, when we talked about it."

"Okay. So it sounds like you've got a problem with a parishioner, and I just wanted to let you know what I'm hearing and give you a heads up."

"Thank you. But really, unless you think it's something a lot of people up here are talking about, I think the real problem is that he's an angry old man who doesn't have the influence he used to have and doesn't have much to keep him busy."

"Well," said the Bishop, "it sounds like you've got a handle on things. Just be careful around Mr. Felder. Other than him, I'm hearing good things about St. Paul's and about your ministry. Anything exciting happening in Lawson?"

Mac laughed, partly in relief that his conversation with the Bishop was nearly over and that there was nothing more serious than cranky old Al Felder to talk about, and partly at the absurdity of thinking that anything exciting might happen in Lawson, Mississippi.

"No, sir, not a thing. I'll let you know when the excitement starts."

Chapter 14

What a World, Huh?

Jeremy was a little late opening Stardust Comics the next morning, but he didn't think anybody was going to mind. Actually, he suspected that nobody would even notice.

His shift at the Hound Dog had ended late the night before, with three big Christmas office parties carrying on late into the night. Mike the manager had talked him into doing his Elvis routine, something he'd promised himself he was never going to do again—but, as Mike said, the longer the customers stayed, the more drinks they ordered, and the more drinks they ordered, the less it mattered that Jeremy's Elvis impersonation left a lot to be desired and the more tips the whole staff could share. "And besides," said Mike, "all you gotta do is go out there, play a little, sing a little, and gyrate a little, while the rest of us'll be cleaning up the kitchen and gettin' ready to close up for the night."

So Jeremy put on the baby blue rhinestone Elvis jumpsuit that Mike used to wear when he could still fit into it, picked up Mike's old Gibson guitar, and went out and played the handful of Elvis songs that he knew. After that, the bosses and their secretaries all asked him to play other Elvis songs that he didn't know—some he'd never even heard of—and he politely declined. He wound up playing the songs he did know again, and that seemed good enough for his well-lubricated audience.

He closed with a rendition of "Blue Christmas" because Rhonda, one of the secretaries at the bank, asked him to sing it. He had protested that he didn't know it, but she was tipsy and told him she'd teach it to him—it seemed pretty clear that the other people from her office really wanted to see that. He'd heard the song before, of course, and he had a rough idea of the tune; he knew some of the words and Rhonda said she knew them all. She did know some of the words he didn't know, and they muddled through it until everybody joined in on the part that everybody seemed to know: "You'll be doin' all right, with your Christmas of white, but I'll have a blue, blue-blue-blue Christmas." It was an instant hit, so they all sang it again.

It was a bit humiliating, but he got a twenty-dollar tip that Rhonda insisted on stuffing into the jumpsuit, as far down as she could get it, which was a little farther than Jeremy thought she should.

He had just unlocked the front door to the comics shop and turned on the light when Tucker came in the back, wearing the Methodist Santa suit.

"You're a pretty skinny Santa."

"Yeah, I've got a pillow in the van."

"You get a bucket and something to hang it on? You get a bell?"

"Yeah, I know this guy, he works with a janitor service, and they clean up at the Salvation Army place where they keep all the Santa stuff. He pinched all that stuff for me; I traded it for a bag of pot, so he's pretty happy."

"So you're going to sell yourself as a Salvation Army bell-ringer?"

"Nah. Tommy—that's my friend—he said I better not do that. He said people try to rip them off all the time, and they get kinda hostile about it. What a world, huh? Think about it: Salvation Army Santas gettin' territorial. So I'm goin' with my own charity."

"The 'Save Grayson Tucker's Sorry Butt from the Savages' Fund?"

"No, man—the 'Strays for Orphans Foundation.'" With that, Tucker led Jeremy out to his van, parked in the back alley, and brought out half a piece of poster board with a picture of a cute child on one side and a picture of a pitiful puppy on the other. Both had big eyes and looked like they were starving; if you looked closely you could see that they were painstakingly cut from a magazine and pasted onto the poster board. Between the pictures, Tucker had carefully written, "Strays and Orphans Deserve Love, Too—Help Us Bring Them Together." Under that was a made-up address, phone number, and website, "just to make it look official." It was actually very well done, Jeremy had to admit.

"You got a tripod?"

"Yeah, but the only kettle the guy had has a big hole through it, see?" Tucker showed him the red kettle with a four-inch rusted-out spot on the bottom and up one side.

"Yeah. Hold on, I got some duct tape—y'know: man's other best friend."

"Red duct tape?"

"No, gray."

"Aw, man—nobody's gonna give to a charity using a kettle that's all duct taped together."

"Just hold on. Lemme see what I can come up with."

Jeremy went into Stardust Comics and in a few minutes came back out with a roll of duct tape, a can of paint, and a screwdriver.

Tucker asked, "So, you got a brush?"

"Well, no, but that's all right."

"How is that all right?"

Jeremy pulled a blue bandana out of the back pocket of his jeans. "Hey, desperate times call for desperate measures, right?" He tore off several sections of tape to close the hole and then opened the can of paint with the screwdriver, which he also used to stir it. "We had this paint from this one time when I tried to paint Superman and Spider-Man playing checkers on the store window."

"Yeah? How did that go?"

Jeremy dipped the bandana into the paint and swabbed it over the duct tape. "Well, they both looked pretty cheesy. I'm thinking painting a rusty kettle with a bandana has got to be easier." He looked at it and swabbed paint over the entire kettle. "Now at least it'll all be the same color."

They looked at it and agreed it looked better than they'd expected. Tucker said, "Man, you got red paint all over your bandana and on your hands."

"Look at all the paint on the ground. Looks like somebody skinned a cat out here or something. It's okay, though—it'll wash off. It's some kind of paint that supposed to be used on the inside of windows, dissolves in water. So, okay. Where you gonna go?"

"Out to the mall, by the entrance to the big department store. Tommy said the Army doesn't usually go down that far."

"You think this is gonna work, Tucker?"

"Yeah, sure. I'll use my winsome good looks and boyish charm, and pretty soon they'll be lining up to give me money."

Tucker could be charming, Jeremy knew. He said, "Well, who knows? Good luck, Santa."

Chapter 15

Justifying and Rationalizing

Little Carlos drove the car through northeast Mississippi in silence. Joey never had much to say, and Mr. C. talked a lot, but only when he needed something. Carlos didn't mind; it gave him time to think about where he was and where he'd been.

He'd come up from a little town in Honduras called Zapotal, running away to the United States of America to find amnesty with his parents and others in the family from the drugs and the gangs and the stifling poverty. There were seventeen of them when they started, as young as his three-year-old niece Lolita and as old as his father's father Don Maximo, who died at the age of eighty-four in the mountains of southern Mexico. Two of his cousins decided to go back to Honduras before they even got through Guatemala; three more decided to stay and find work in Mexico City. Carlos's older brother Jorge was shot and killed by a coyote, a Mexican who made his living by extorting preposterous amounts of money to smuggle people across the border in the back of a truck. They buried him in a wilderness somewhere and scratched his name into a rock they put over the pile of dry dirt covering his body. Carlos and his father had to drag his screaming mother away from the grave.

The ten remaining pilgrims waded the Rio Grande early one morning on foot, nearly eight months after they'd left Honduras. Carlos's Uncle Miguel and two more cousins were caught by immigration agents and sent back into Mexico; his parents and sisters stayed in New Mexico, looking for work and searching for a safe place for their family.

Carlos and his cousin Big Carlos (Little Carlos was actually an inch taller than Big Carlos, but Big Carlos had a better appetite even as a child and outweighed him by at least forty pounds) wanted to go farther into the States and farther away from the border agents. It had been a dream of Little Carlos's mother to see Elvis Presley, so with no more compelling reason than that, the two of them made their way east, crossing the Mississippi River at Memphis, Tennessee. They went to Graceland, where they were disappointed to hear that the King had been dead for years.

It was Big Carlos who found a connection to a group of men in a warehouse by the river who stole expensive cars and either sold them quickly or disassembled them and sold the parts. Big Carlos had been trying to make his living as a mechanic back home; now he discovered that taking cars apart was much easier and much more lucrative than trying to fix them. It was Big Carlos who brought Little Carlos into the operation as a driver. Little Carlos was a quick learner. Even though he spoke almost no English at first, it didn't take long for them to show him how to break into a car, disable the alarm system, hot-wire it, and drive it to the warehouse.

The hardest part for both cousins had been justifying and rationalizing what they were doing. They'd never been criminals before—part of the reason they'd left Honduras was so they wouldn't have to be. After several long conversations, they agreed to believe that the fancy cars they stole and stripped belonged to rich Americans who had expensive insurance policies that would pay them back, so it was just a matter of inconvenience for the car owners. For the cousins, it was a matter of having money to send to their families back in Honduras and enough to send to those they'd left behind in New Mexico, who had discovered it wasn't as easy to find a job there as they had been led to believe.

"Carlos."

"Yes, Boss?"

"Pull over next time you get a chance. I gotta pee."

"Yes, Boss. Next place I see."

Joey perked up at the prospect of stopping. "Hey, Boss?"

"Yeah?"

"You think maybe we could get somethin' to eat? I'm starving."

"Yeah, it looks like you're just wasting away up there. Yeah, okay—let's stop and grab a bite. Carlos, where the hell are we?"

"I don't know, Boss—last sign I saw was for Potts Camp. Three, four miles back."

That meant New Albany was less than twenty miles ahead, and Vinnie had no intention of ever going back to his hometown. "There's a barbecue joint outside Hickory Flat—we can stop there."

Carlos said, "Yes sir, Boss."

Joey said, "I love barbecue."

Vinnie said nothing, but his conviction echoed in his mind: "I am never going back to New Albany, Mississippi."

Chapter 16

A Frigate Under Full Sail

Mac locked the door to the St. Paul's offices behind him and started walking toward Fuddy's. It was only about five blocks; he told himself the walk would do him as much good as the caffeine. It was a crisp December day, a little chilly but the sun was shining.

As he was about to pass in front of the post office, he saw with some dismay that Mrs. Ralph Ketchum was just coming out of it, and he stopped to reconsider the next few minutes of his life. A conversation with Mrs. Ketchum took some preparation.

When Mac had been in the process of moving to St. Paul's, in a preliminary meeting with the head of the search committee and the Senior Warden, Mac had told them what he'd thought was an amusing anecdote about a man in his previous parish who seemed to take delight in being righteously indignant about almost everything. After the two other men had shared a quick, uncomfortable glance, Mac had done a little fishing: "Well, I suppose he might not be the only person who enjoys being offended."

Reluctantly, they'd told him about Mrs. Ralph Ketchum in almost reverential tones, always referring to her as "Mrs. Ketchum." He'd asked what her first name was, but they said didn't know—they agreed that in theory she must have one, but nowadays she was introduced as Mrs. Ralph Ketchum, and that was about as far as anybody ever got. One of them thought Mr. Ralph Ketchum had been dead for more than thirty years, but as far as he knew, she was strictly Mrs. Ralph Ketchum, apparently on a first-name basis with no one.

She had been the chair of the St. Paul's altar guild for decades and still kept her eye on things, making sure everything was just the way it was supposed to be, which was the way she'd done it and the way it had always been done. She had been the parish treasurer for more than twenty years, until the priest before Mac had insisted that the church records be kept on computer, which Mrs. Ketchum simply could not abide. She kept close watch over who was wearing what to Sunday morning services and felt no compunction about speaking to a young person's parents if they were not attired to her standards. The kids in the youth group referred to her as "Triple-A C": Avoid At All Costs. Mac assumed that a majority of the parish would not likely disagree.

She was also the single largest contributor to the parish budget, a fact that she made sure Mac and everyone else did not forget. With Mrs. Ralph Ketchum, as with many other people with wealth and influence, the money came with strings attached. In Mrs. Ketchum's case, the strings were more like heavy cords, getting close to ropes. She had become an unspoken step in the parish's decision-making process: a) Here's an idea, b) Would it further the mission of the church, c) Do we have the resources to do it, and d) What would Mrs. Ralph Ketchum think?

Nor was her influence limited to the parish. She and her husband had so judiciously and strategically spread their wealth, or at least a fraction of the accrued interest on the wealth that Mr. Ketchum had inherited, that their name was all over Lawson: the Ketchum Bleachers were on the visitors' side at the high school football stadium, the Ketchum Conference Room was in the Lawson city library, and Ketchum Park had been built over the old public swimming pool when the city fathers claimed that desegregation had forced them to fill it in.

Mac took it as part of his cross to bear that he would have to talk to Mrs. Ketchum when they were at the parish, but he thought it unfair to require him to deal with her out on the street; he was looking for some way out when she turned and saw him.

"Good morning, Father McBride."

"Good morning, Mrs. Ketchum."

"Out Christmas shopping, Father?"

"No, just out for a stroll, taking a break from working on a couple of sermons. Christmas is on a Monday this year, so I have a sermon for Sunday morning and another for the Christmas Eve service that night."

She said flatly, "I'm sure that must be interesting." She didn't complete the sentence, but he could hear her unspoken conclusion: "to someone else."

He said, "Are you out picking up a few last-minute things?"

"Good heavens, no. I've already shopped and mailed the presents I needed on the line." She noticed his puzzled face and tried again: "On the computer, on the webthing, on the line."

"Oh. Yes, it seems that shopping online is very convenient."

"That's as may be, I'm sure. It all seems very impersonal to me."

"Yes, ma'am, that's what I think, too. I think I'll go to the bookstore at the mall and pick up what I need . . ."

"Yes, all very interesting, I'm sure, but I must run."

"Yes, ma'am. It's always good to see you. Merry Christmas."

Mac breathed a sigh of relief and was just about to continue walking when he realized that Mrs. Ralph Ketchum had already started her one-woman parade, making its way with deliberate dignity in the same direction as his, towards Fuddy's. He didn't want to say goodbye to her and then pass her on the sidewalk, so he stood awkwardly for a moment, then decided to step into the post office. There was a long line of people waiting to mail Christmas packages, which he felt gave him a plausible excuse to go back out to the street. Then he realized that he wasn't holding anything he could have pretended to mail, so it was all completely silly.

He stepped back out and looked up the street, seeing that Mrs. Ketchum hadn't gotten very far, less than half a block. She was a frigate under full sail, but she was carrying a full cargo. He decided he could cross the street, walk up a few blocks, and then cross back over to Fuddy's. In front of Milligan's, the town's old hardware and sporting goods store, he was stopped again.

"Mac!"

Early Miller was a local attorney with a modest practice, which was apparently how he liked it. He wasn't actually a member of the parish, but he'd played baseball in high school and was a ringer for the St. Paul's men's softball team. The two had become friends, as long as they stayed away from church or politics and talked about sports or movies. Early was a big fan of Hollywood. "Hey, Early, how're you doing?"

"Fair to partly cloudy at the moment, Mac. Actually, I've been meaning to have a chat. I'm afraid I have a bone to pick with you."

This was new territory; they'd never had a serious conversation before. "Oh. Is that a little bone, or one that I might choke on?"

"No, it's just something that's been bothering me. Maybe the size of a bone is in the throat of the beholder."

"I guess so. Hey, listen, I'm on my way to Fuddy's—I'll buy you a cup of coffee, we can sit down, and you can pick your bone."

"If you throw in a piece of lemon pie, that bone might just go away altogether."

"Deal! Man, if I'd known I could dissolve bones people wanted to pick with me with a piece of pie, I'd have . . ."

"You'd have what?"

"I guess I'd have bought a lot of pies by now."

They waited for a car to pass before stepping out into Jefferson Street, just as Mac saw Mrs. Ralph Ketchum entering Fuddy's Pie Emporium. He said, "Hold on, Early."

Chapter 17

Trying to Explain
Magnetism to a Mouse

Forgive her father? Narni was indignant. This old guy was telling her to forgive her drug addict father, the man who'd murdered her mother and abandoned her to the foster system? The hell she would! She didn't know what was going on, but she sure as hell knew this crazy person didn't have anything to do with God—not the God who said "Thou shalt not kill," not the God who said, "An eye for an eye, a tooth for a tooth." Narni didn't know who the old man was or how he knew all the things he seemed to know, but she was certain of one thing: he sure as hell wasn't God.

She folded her arms across her chest defensively.

Miss Mully leaned toward her and said, "Hold on now, Sweet Pea. It ain't hurtin' your daddy one bit, you hatin' him like this. You the one gettin' all chewed up, an' it ain't hurtin' him at all." Narni glared at her.

The old woman's smooth face was full of love as she looked across the table at the Old Man in the gray cardigan. "Lord, why are You here?"

"Mary Elizabeth, you could not stand to know all the reasons I Am here. I Am here in part for the pie, I must admit. I Am here to meet with My son who was with me a few minutes ago. But I am here for Narni as well, and for you, and for Walter. I have more reasons, but that is enough for the moment."

"Lord, you remember my daughter?"

"Tallulah Mae. She will welcome you Home before too long. She is a beautiful soul, just like her mother."

"When will . . . I come there?"

"You have more life to live here before you come Home."

"Lord, I want to know why—why she had to . . . why she was born like that, and why she . . . why she had to die like that? That has 'sturbed me, Lord—and I . . . I want to know why."

"Yes, I know. This is a difficult thing for you and for many others: it is in your nature to know enough to ask why, but you are not able to understand the answers to the questions you ask."

Mary Elizabeth was disappointed and made no effort to hide it. She turned to Walter and asked, "What d'you think He mean by that, Dub?"

Walter mumbled, "I don't have no idea."

The Old Man continued with infinite patience: "Some of what you ask is like trying to explain magnetism to a mouse. The mouse is simply not able to understand."

Walter whispered, "He sayin' you like a mouse now, askin' sumpin' you got no business askin'."

The Old Man laughed again, and despite herself, Narni thrilled at the sound of it. The sound of his laughter was like Christmas morning when she was a child, finding her stocking filled with gifts and candies and presents under the tree, and her mom and dad holding hands, and the smell of turkey in the oven and dressing and pecan pie—it was home and hope and life and love. It was joy.

"No, Walter. You have every right to ask the questions. You just are not able to fully understand the answers."

Even though his response was kind and loving and patient, it made Narni furious. It seemed so condescending. She was not feeling so kind or loving and was rapidly losing her patience. "Just give us a chance! Can't you try to explain it to us mere mortals?"

The Old Man looked at Narni, recognizing and accepting her frustration. He said, "Mary Elizabeth's daughter Tallulah Mae was born with cerebral palsy, diminished intellectual capacity, and a faulty valve in her heart. She never walked. she never talked, except to call her mother Mully, her only word. But she loved her mother, and her mother loved her and cared for her every day of her short life. She died of heart failure when she was sixteen years old." He turned to Mary Elizabeth, and said, "I know that caused you a great deal of unbearable pain, my dear child."

Mary Elizabeth whispered, "It broke my heart, Lord."

"Yes, I know. I know it did. I have felt your pain."

"But why, Lord? Why did she have to . . . have to be born like that? Why couldn't You fix her?"

The Old Man sighed deeply, as if He were absorbing Mary Elizabeth's pain. He said, "Because the world is made the way it is. The world is made for you, for the children of God, and you are given free will. That is what it means to be made in the image of God: you are given the freedom and the burden of choosing."

Mary Elizabeth said, "I didn't choose none of that."

"No, you did not."

Walter spoke up. "So why the little girl was born like that, the way she was?"

"This is the part that is difficult for you to understand. I made the world as it is so that you can be free, to choose good or evil, love or hate."

Walter said, "But You said it was all good. In that Bible story, you said it was all good."

"Yes, and it is. But part of the goodness of Creation is that you have the freedom to make choices. It is no freedom if all you have to choose from is one good or another good."

Narni, Mary Elizabeth, and Walter didn't know what to say, and wisely said nothing. The Old Man continued, "In order for you to be truly free to choose, there must be some things that are good and other things that are not. In order for you to choose between faith and fear, there must be reasons for you to doubt. It is much more important for you to believe than it is for you to understand."

Walter said, "This right here is why so many folks ain't believin' they is a God no more. It don't make no sense."

"You want it to make sense so that you can believe. But the truth is that you have to believe for anything to make sense. What you believe cannot be limited by what you understand."

Mary Elizabeth nodded, and Walter looked down into his coffee cup with no expression on his face. But Narni was having none of it. "Does that explain why a little girl is born with cerebral palsy? Is that why there are earthquakes? Or why people are killed for no damn reason at all? Does it explain why . . ." She faltered, out of energy and unwilling to expose the deep question of her existence.

"Why your father killed your mother? No. No explanation could be sufficient to ease that pain. Only love and faith can ever truly mend your heart."

Narni blurted it out before she could stop herself: "But why? If you're supposed to be God, if you're all high and mighty—if you're all perfect and powerful and you made the world—why does all this bad stuff happen all the time?"

"In your own experience, you know that you have to endure sour to cherish sweet. You have to know the dark to see light. If all of creation is simply and only good, then you would not know it to be good. For Creation to be complete, it must exist with all degrees of what you think of as good and bad, sweet and sour, light and dark."

Narni looked at the Old Man and quoted a passage from *Moby Dick*, one of her favorite books: "Truly to enjoy bodily warmth, some small part of you must be cold, for there is no quality in this world that is not what it is merely by contrast."

He said, "Exactly. This delicious lemon icebox pie would not be nearly so good if it were only sweet or only sour—it is those things together that make it wonderful."

Mary Elizabeth murmured, "Yea, the darkness hideth not from thee; but the night shineth as the day: the darkness and the light are both alike to thee." Narni looked at her, wondering, as the older woman continued, "Somewhere in one of them Psalms, I believe."

Chapter 18

Swallowed Up by the Shadows

Jeremy had just started his shift at the Hound Dog. He'd called Narni at least ten times that afternoon while he was sitting at the comics shop, but she hadn't answered. He told himself that all he wanted was to tell her how sorry he was, but really all he wanted was for her to tell him that she still loved him. When the all-Elvis-all-the-time jukebox played "Heartbreak Hotel," it was all he could do to keep washing dishes:

> Well, since my baby left me,
> Well, I found a new place to dwell:
> Well, it's down at the end of Lonely Street
> at Heartbreak Hotel.
> Well, I get so lonely, baby,
> I get so lonely, I get so lonely I could die.

When he carried a bag of garbage to the dumpster, Tucker stepped out of the dark, from out of nowhere. Jeremy had never seen him so agitated, so frantic and scared. At first, he was concerned that Tucker would see that he'd been crying, but he soon remembered that he didn't need to worry about that at all—Tucker never saw much past himself. Tucker whispered, "Hey, man. Look, are there any strangers in the restaurant tonight?"

"Hey. Um, I don't know. I just got here a few minutes ago, and I've been washing dishes in the kitchen the whole time. Why?"

"Just watch out for these guys from Memphis for me, would you?"

"Um, sure. Why would they come to the Hound Dog? What do they look like?"

"They know I'm here—where else you gonna eat in Lawson? You'll see Joey first. He's a big, tall guy, hair cut short, looks like he could put his head through a brick wall and not feel a thing. He'll be with the driver, a little guy from Mexico or someplace. They work for Vinnie Carlisle, he's the boss. He's got dark hair greased back, always wears a dark suit, has a stupid-looking moustache. He gives the orders, and they do what he tells them to do."

"Is this like the Mob or something?"

"Yeah, something like that."

"Aw, man—are you crazy? What're you doing with people like that?"

"Well, I had to borrow some money from Vinnie to pay off this other guy, you know?"

"What other guy?"

"That older guy. Luke something, his last name starts with a P, I think—I don't remember now. He runs a card game in downtown Memphis, tough customer. I thought I was winning, I thought I had these guys. And I let myself get trapped. I bet more than I could afford to lose, and then I thought the only way to get the money to pay 'em was to keep playing. Finally, I told all those guys I had to pee and climbed out of the bathroom window. The game was on the second floor of this old building, and I sort of jumped and sort of fell. I could have died, man!"

"Jesus! It sounds like you still might!"

"Yeah."

"So how much did you get in your Santa suit?"

"I did okay, I guess. I got almost three hundred dollars. This one old lady gave me a check for a hundred more, but she made it out to the Strays for Orphans Foundation, so I need to figure out how I can cash it."

"So you've still got seventy-seven hundred to go? And the Mob is after you?"

"Yeah. Well, I woulda done better if I coulda stayed longer, but the Salvation Army truck came around and said they were going to call the police on me. They looked pretty pissed. Hey, listen, man— thanks for trying to help. I brought the suit back for the Methodists. Not the beard and the hat, though. I need to hold on to them for

SWALLOWED UP BY THE SHADOWS

a little while, you mind?" Tucker gave Jeremy the white box labeled "Santa Suit."

"What're you gonna do?"

"I don't know, man, I don't know. But I'd rather get the crap kicked out of me than go to Cincinnati and pretend I'm somebody I can't be."

Jeremy had been trying not to say this next part, but he just couldn't help it. "I've, uh—listen: I've got a couple hundred saved up. I could let you borrow it, you know? I've been saving up for a ring, but it doesn't look like I'm going to be needing it now."

Tucker was genuinely touched by the offer and was glad that Jeremy was his friend. "Thanks, man—I appreciate it. But I'm gonna need a lot more than that. Keep your money, buy the ring, marry your girl, and don't worry about me. I'll be fine; I always am."

Jeremy was relieved that his offer was refused, but he knew he would have given Tucker the money if it would have helped him. "So . . . um . . . what can I—?"

"You can't help me now. I just gotta do what I gotta do."

"But what are you gonna do?"

"I . . . hey, look—I gotta go. I'll see you around."

And then Tucker was gone, swallowed up by the shadows. Jeremy stood there with a box full of Santa wondering what would happen to his friend. It wasn't until he was washing dishes again that he wondered why Tucker had kept the Santa's beard and jolly red hat.

Chapter 19

Faster Than His Shoe

Vinnie Carlisle, Joey Carolla, and Little Carlos rolled down Main
Street into Lawson, Mississippi, just in time to see young Lieutenant
Joseph O. Durning Jr. step out of the town's only police cruiser
with his sidearm drawn and pointed at the Bank of Lawson. The
policeman crouched behind the door of his vehicle and shouted,
"Come out! We've got the bank surrounded! Come out with your
hands up!"—just like you see on TV.

Joey said, "Looks like somebody's robbin' the bank, Boss."

Vinnie snorted. "Idiots. How much money could there be in a
dumpy little town like this?"

Little Carlos had slowed the car to a crawl in the middle of the
street, not wanting to get too close to the flashing blue lights. "What
do you want me to do, Boss?"

"Find a place to park. I want to know what's going on here."

Carlos found a place down a side street and parked the car; Mr.
C. told him and Joey to stay with the car while he did a little looking
around. They'd been there for less than two minutes when a man
wearing a Santa hat and a white beard careened past them. Carlos
noticed that he was missing one of his shoes because it made him
run funny and because his bare foot was bloody. It looked like he was
running away at full speed, like he was scared of whatever he'd left
behind. Carlos and Joey watched as the guy ran past them without
sparing them a glance, until he took a left, parallel to the main street
of the town. Carlos thought about commenting to Joey on what
they'd just seen but decided there was no real point.

A few minutes later Vinnie came back. "Seems like the Bank of
Lawson was just robbed by a skinny Santa!"

Joey turned to Little Carlos, amazed. "What, that guy we just
saw?"

"Yeah, man—must have been." Carlos turned to Vinnie and said, "Yeah, Boss—we saw this dude wearin' a Santa hat and a beard. He ran right past us, right here! He was goin' fast, too—I think he ran faster than his shoe or something, y'know?"

Vinnie was calculating, looking to see how this could profit him. After a moment he said, "Did you see which way he went?"

"Yeah, Boss. He ran down that way and took a left."

"Was he a white guy or a black guy?"

Carlos accepted the fact that those were the only two likely choices: the possibility of the running man being a Latino was pretty slim in Lawson, Mississippi. He said, "He was a white dude."

"You think he could've been our boy Tucker?"

Little Carlos said, "Who?"

"The guy we're down here to see. The guy that owes me eight grand."

"Oh. I never seen that guy, Boss."

"What about you, Joey? You've seen Tucker, right?"

"Yeah, Boss, I seen him."

"Well, you think the guy you saw might be the guy we're here to see?"

"I don't know, Boss. Maybe. He was goin' pretty fast, and he had that beard and Santa hat and everything . . . could be, I don't know. Maybe."

Vinnie looked at Carlos and held up a hand to indicate Tucker's height. "About this tall?"

Little Carlos said, "Sí."

Vinnie continued, "Skinny guy? Scared look in his eyes?"

Carlos repeated, "Sí."

Vinnie made a decision. "All right. Let's follow the Santa and see where he leads us. I bet he ain't goin' to the North Pole!"

Chapter 20

Love Is Not Proven

Narni said, "I don't understand."

The Old Man smiled wistfully and said, "I know. It is not for you to understand. That is why it is so much more important for you to believe, because you will not ever be able to fully understand. You know the universe is infinite, do you not? But you are not able to understand infinity. What is beyond the stars but more stars, and more beyond them, forever?"

Narni felt the goosebumps on her arms and asked in an awed whisper, "Who are you, really?"

He nodded before answering, "I Am who I Am. Who you believe Me to be is for you to decide. I will not determine your choices. Ask Mary Elizabeth. Ask Walter."

Mary Elizabeth said with confidence, "He is the Lord God." Walter was less eloquent but no less sure: "He mus' be Jesus."

Narni hesitated. It was so easy for them, unburdened by complexity or skepticism, not needing proof. She said, "I . . . I want to believe, I do. But—"

"Yes, I know," the Old Man said. "It is a struggle to believe something you are not able to comprehend."

That was it, exactly. "Yes, sir." And then, hesitantly, she added, "Thank you for understanding."

And then He continued. "And yet you loved your mother. You believe she loved you."

Narni was instantly incensed. "What the hell does that have to do with anything?"

"Bear with me, Sweet Heart. You know you loved your mother, and you know she loved you as well."

"Of course I did!"

"That is something you would say you are sure of."

"Yes!"

"You would say you know it?"

"What? How could you say something like—"

"And you have proof?"

"What?"

"You know that your mother loved you because you can prove it? You can prove that you loved her?"

"No!" Narni was confused and off balance. "I loved her because she was my mother. She loved me because . . . because she just loved me."

"Yes, she did. She still does. But I Am talking about proof. Can you prove her love for you or your love for her?"

"You are talking about my mother and questioning whether she really loved me, or whether I really loved her. You don't know anything about my mother! You don't know anything about me! I don't have to prove anything to you!"

Mary Elizabeth put her hand on Narni's hand, soothing. "Hush, Sweet Pea. Just let the Man talk. You might need to hear what He is sayin.'"

"Narni, I do not mean to be harsh. I Am trying to make an important point. I know that your mother loved you very much and loves you still. And I know that you love her very, very much. What I want you to understand is that love is not about proof, ever. Love is trusted, love is believed, but Love is not proved or disproved."

Narni thought about this for a minute as the others at the table watched and waited. Then she said, "So what does that mean? What does any of that have to do with me?"

The Old Man smiled, and Narni thought for a moment that she could believe it was the smile of the Soul of Kindness. He said, "You are free to believe that I Am the Creator, or you may believe I Am just an old fool. You may believe I Am both. That is, after all, what this child of mine believes."

The Old Man nodded toward the front door, where the young man who'd been with him earlier was walking toward them. Narni had not heard the bell at the door jingle, but he was there anyway: the Dangerous Man had returned.

Chapter 21

A Head Full of Soggy Cotton

If Tucker had been honest with himself (a practice he tended to avoid if at all possible), he'd have known that trying to raise the money ringing a bell at Christmas shoppers wasn't going to work, but it seemed better than doing nothing at all. He had just been hoping, hoping that something would go right for him just this once.

And despite his best efforts at self-deception, he knew that trying to rob the Bank of Lawson was going to be even more foolish, even as he tried to convince himself that robbing banks was considered honorable, heroic in some circles. They'd written songs about Bonnie and Clyde . . .

He'd spent all of Thursday night and most of the money he'd collected as a Santa fraud in the Bluebell, a largely gay bar in Tupelo, trying to enjoy one last evening before facing whatever today would bring. He'd been looking for inspiration, looking for some other way out, looking for the nerve it would take to play his next role as a bank robber.

He'd slept late, not wanting to wake up, not wanting to face the danger and desperation of the day. Then he'd taken a shower, gotten dressed, and walked right into the Bank of Lawson before he could talk himself out of it, bold as a drunk frat boy at homecoming, wearing the Santa hat and beard for a disguise.

If there was ever a plan to start with, things did not go according to it.

First there was a line at both of the tellers' windows. He'd gone in with the hat and beard already on so nobody would see his face, but that meant he had to stand in line for a few minutes looking like a Yuletide fool. Still, that was all right: it was Christmas time; he was just a customer who was really into the spirit of the season. It wasn't until he was next in line that he realized the teller was a young man he thought he vaguely remembered meeting the night before at the

Bluebell. He wasn't sure (there had been what seemed like several gallons of tequila), but it looked like him. Tucker was hoping that if it was him, he wouldn't recognize . . .

"Tucker! Oh my God! I almost didn't recognize you wearing all this Santa regalia. How precious!"

He couldn't remember the young man's name, and wondered what else he couldn't remember from the night before. He looked at the man's Bank of Lawson Employee nametag and whispered, "Look, Carson—I'm sorry—this is so awkward . . . but this is a stickup."

Tucker did remember the young man's exaggerated laugh from the night before when he heard it again from across the teller's counter. "Oh, you're too funny! How did you even know I worked here?"

"No, I'm serious. I have to rob this bank. Can you just empty all the money out of your drawer or something?"

"You gonna show me your gun, Desperado?"

Now Tucker was panicking. Some of the other people standing in the lines around him were sure to notice something was wrong. "Give me all the money in your drawer," he hissed. "Now."

Carson stared at him, not laughing now. "You're serious?"

Tucker tried and failed to keep the shrill out of his voice. "Yes, I'm serious!" His voice went even shriller: "Give me the money. Be quick and be quiet."

Tucker watched as the young teller's hand slowly slid under the counter; there seemed to be little he could do about it. The alarm was silent within the bank, but Tucker felt its impact, as the eyes of all the managers and tellers seemed to converge on him in the next moment. Even the old bank guard woke up from a short winter's nap to wonder what was going on.

Tucker knew the moment was collapsing on him. "Give me the money!" As soon as he said it, he knew he'd spoken too loudly.

The young man with the artificial laugh was deadly serious now, all the warmth gone icy in his eyes. "Or what, Desperado? You gonna shoot me?"

In the part of his mind that was still trying to make sense of things, Tucker had known it was dumb to try to rob a bank without a gun—his problem was that the rational part had not been the part of his mind making decisions lately. He'd thought about getting a gun; he hadn't decided against it, but in all the foggy desperation and the cloudy aftershock of tequila, he hadn't done anything about getting one. Now—too late—he had to concede that you can't really rob a bank without a gun. He was in the process of forming the excuses he needed to tell himself ("Well, I've never robbed a bank before . . .") when Carson leaned over the counter and whispered, "You need to run away now, Tucker."

Tucker knew he wasn't thinking clearly. It was like he had a head full of soggy cotton, and he couldn't seem to make himself focus. "Run away?" he murmured.

Some of the warmth returned to the teller's eyes, Tucker thought, or it might have been pity. He whispered a little more urgently, "Run away *now*, Tucker!"

So Tucker ran toward the front door, which was being blocked by the old bank guard.

Chapter 22

A Little Nonsense Now and Then

Mac felt like he'd painted himself into something of a corner. He'd already had all the conversation with Mrs. Ralph Ketchum that he needed for the day, honestly a little more than he wanted, but she had just stepped into Fuddy's, right after he'd told Early Miller that he would buy him a cup of coffee and a piece of pie. Some days you just can't win, he thought.

Mac thought surely she wouldn't be in there for long; Mrs. Ketchum didn't seem the type to chat idly or linger in a public place for longer than absolutely necessary. Maybe he could wait her out.

There was a little concrete bench near the spot where they were standing, placed there by the Daughters of the Confederacy to mark the spot where something had happened during the War. Whatever it was must have seemed important at some point, but now it was mostly forgotten. Mac gestured toward the bench, and they went and sat down. After a moment, he said to Early, "Tell me about this bone of yours."

"What, and let you wiggle out of buying me a piece of pie?"

"No, I just thought . . . that if it's something sensitive, it might be better if we're not sitting in the middle of a bunch of people. You know how crowded Fuddy's can be, and with it being almost Christmas and all, I just thought maybe—"

"No, it's nothing like that. I'm not talking about making a confession or something, Father."

"Good. I don't think either one of us would have enough time to hear your confession all in one sitting."

Both men laughed, relieved for their own reasons, and Early said, "Yeah, no—it would probably take a couple of hours because I'd have to explain a lot of it to you."

"Heh—touché. So what's your bone?"

"I'm still getting the pie, right?"

"Absolutely."

"Well, I guess it's not really a bone to pick with you particularly, but with the whole church. Or maybe just the Catholics."

"So that narrows it down a little, huh? About half the Christians in the world are Roman Catholics."

"It's about the Virgin Mary."

"Okay."

"This messes me up every year, every Christmas."

They sat in uneasy silence for a moment, until Mac prompted, "Okay—what about Mary messes you up?"

"Well . . . you know I grew up Catholic, right?"

"Yeah."

"Well, you know I don't go to church all that much, right?"

"I know you've come to St. Paul's a couple of times, and we're always glad to see you."

"Well, the reason I don't come all that much is because I . . . well, I just couldn't . . . I just can't stand the way they talk about the Virgin Mary, and it made me think the whole deal is just a bunch of baloney." Early took a deep breath, relieved that he'd said out loud something that had bothered him since he was a child. He looked over at Mac for condemnation, or to see if he was shocked.

Mac nodded his encouragement and gently asked, "What is it that you have such a hard time with?"

"I mean, she did what God asked her to do and everything, but it's like they're making her out to be a goddess or something."

The priest said, "Hey, look, Early: you grew up Catholic, and there are folks in that system who might be a little out of balance about the Virgin Mary. I grew up in the Episcopal Church, and we've got people out of balance, too. We have people who are out of whack about the stained glass windows, or the tradition, or the illusion that We've Always Done It That Way. All those church folks—all those Catholics and Episcopalians and Methodists and Presbyterians— we're all just people. Most of us are doing the best we can. Some of the time, anyway."

"But they made it sound like Mary was like, part of God or something."

"And that's not what you believe."

"No! Nobody should believe that!"

"Well, hold on there, cowboy. If you're ticked off that somebody is saying you have to believe something, you can't really say that nobody should believe what they believe. Right? I mean, you've been upset—"

"I'm not upset!"

"Okay, you've been mildly distressed for a long time because you felt like somebody was trying to make you believe something you didn't want to believe, right?"

"Well, that's part of it. I mean—I really admire the Virgin Mary; it took a lot of courage to believe what the angel told her and all that. But to make her out to be sort of like a goddess or something—I mean, she was just a kid, right? It makes me wonder if the whole thing was made up."

"Like the Easter Bunny?"

"Yeah. Well, no. That's kinda fun, y'know—that's for kids. But this business about Mary and Jesus and God and all that, that's serious, y'know? What if I don't believe any of this stuff, Mac? That's like, that's what happens after we die and stuff—that's what all this church and God and faith stuff is really all about, right?"

Mac thought for a few seconds. "Yeah, it's serious. Maybe it's better to say it's important. But I think maybe it's not like that."

"Like what?"

"I don't think the whole purpose of being religious is just to save ourselves from the wrath of God."

"Oh." Early Miller was not by nature a serious person, and he was surprised to find himself enjoying this conversation. Now he had to think a moment before he said, "So what *is* the purpose of being religious?"

Mac answered, "I think the whole point is to help us love God and love each other. I think a big part of it is so we can love ourselves. I think we mess up the whole thing when we mix it up with the threat of Hell, or when we encourage people to live in shame or guilt."

Early grinned. "So you think some of the stuff the church teaches is of full of baloney, too, right?"

Mac laughed. "Yeah, I guess so." They sat in companionable silence for a few seconds, then Mac said, "A heresy is an idea or an argument against the doctrine of the church. I'm not too worried about heresy—a little bit of heresy is good for the church; keeps us on our toes." Early looked skeptical, so Mac added, "You know, it's like Thomas Jefferson said: 'I hold it that a little rebellion now and then is a good thing, and as necessary in the political world as storms in the physical.'" Mac smiled to himself; it was one of his favorite quotes, and he was glad he'd remembered the whole thing.

Early replied, "A little nonsense now and then is relished by the wisest men."

Mac was impressed; he'd never thought of Early as a deep thinker. "Wow—who said that?"

"Willy Wonka."

They both laughed and sat, basking in the sun on a cool day, enjoying the moment. Mac had been watching the door at Fuddy's for the last few minutes, and either he'd missed Mrs. Ketchum coming out or she was still in there. Either way, it was time for some coffee. He said, "C'mon, my fellow heretic—let's go get some pie."

Chapter 23

Pleased to Make Your 'Quaintance

Mary Elizabeth gasped when she saw the young man dressed in black approaching the table. "You! What are *you* doing here?"

The Adversary of God was surprisingly gentle and respectful. "I am here because He asked me here." Then, turning to the Old Man, he continued, "Lord, I regret that I let my desire to protect You cause me to leave earlier. I have returned now if You still wish to talk to me."

"Thank you, Ben. I Am glad you have come back and always glad for us to talk. I have always wished it so."

"Yeah, I know. It's just that this . . . this arrangement is just so . . . it sickens me."

"I know. I wish it were not the case for you. Perhaps you would not find the humans so repulsive if you talked with them."

"Talked with . . . ?"

"Yes. Would that be so terrible? Whether you like it or not, they are My children too, just as you are. It will surely do you no harm to listen to a few of them for a short while. They may surprise you."

When Satan spoke again, it was in a smaller voice, almost pleading. "Oh Lord, I don't want to. Please don't make me."

"Of course I will not force you to do this. I simply suggest; I encourage My children to do what is right. I do not force. But what is there to fear? No harm will come to you. It may be, as you imagine, a waste of time, but what is time to you and Me?"

The Adversary of God turned to his left to regard Miss Mully, now known as Mary Elizabeth. He looked at her suspiciously, the same way someone might look at a piece of fish to see if it's gone bad. Mary Elizabeth, who had recently started feeling better than she'd been for years, spat out, "What the hell are *you* looking at?"

The Prince of Hell swallowed, his Adam's apple bobbing down and up in a very appealing way, Narni thought. "Madame, please allow me to introduce myself. I am Ben Shachar."

"I know who you are. You're the Devil, the Antichrist. You're the Beast in the Book of Revelations, and your number is six-six-six. I know *exactly* who *you* are."

His face grew dark and for a moment seemed not as attractive as Narni had thought. The Old Man put His hand on the younger man's arm and spoke to him gently: "Just try."

He took a deep, shuddering breath and quietly said to the homeless woman, "Yes, madame, I am Satan, the Adversary of God. This has been my role, my privilege, and my curse for longer than even I can remember. But I am not the Antichrist or the Beast of John's Revelation, and I have no number. That is nothing more than a peculiar and imaginative jumble of myth and fiction."

Narni was startled. All of this had been way too weird for a long while, and now it had gotten much, much weirder. Everybody looked at her when she gasped, and now—feeling like she was expected to say something—she asked, "You're the Devil?" She turned to the Old Man. "But you said his name is Ben."

"Yes," said the Lord of Heaven and Earth. "The Hebrew prophet Isaiah called him Helel ben Shachar, Shining One, or Son of the Morning. 'Ben' is a Hebrew form of 'Son of,' I call him Ben to remind him that he is my son. Even before Lucifer chose to leave My heavenly court, his role was to be Satan, My adversary."

"But why?"

"Because I need an adversary."

Walter spoke up. "This about dark and light, and sweet and sour and all that?"

Narni thought the Old Man's smile was like the lights coming back on after a storm had knocked out the electricity for a few hours. "Yes, Walter, precisely. Even I make choices; even I choose between what is good and what is evil."

"He says it keeps Him on His toes, so to speak," added Satan. "Keeps Him honest."

They sat quietly for more than a minute, each of them unwilling to say anything for their own reasons. Finally, Ben, who seemed most obviously uncomfortable with the silence, turned to Mary Elizabeth and said, "I am as you see me, madame: the Adversary of God."

"And now you just talkin' to me, like I was . . . what, like you my friend or sumpin'?"

The Adversary looked at the Old Man, who nodded reassuringly, like a mother encouraging her toddler to jump into a swimming pool for the first time. Then, reluctantly, he answered her, "I . . . I don't know. I don't know about friends. I don't think I've ever . . . I can't say I've ever had one."

Mary Elizabeth looked stunned, clearly thinking that life without friends would be desolate indeed. She said, "But Gabriel, or Michael, or . . ."

Walter offered helpfully, "Or Ralph?"

The Old Man said, "Raphael."

At this, the Adversary of God smiled. It was not a normal facial expression for him, and it forced his face to go into unaccustomed shapes. The lines on his face tried to turn it into a sneer or a smirk, but it was a smile all the same. It seemed to Narni that he was trying to hold it back, but he couldn't: Satan smiled. He said, "Gabriel and Michael and . . . Ralph are my brothers. We have been competitive for a very long time. But no"—the smile faded—"we are *not* friends."

This exchange dislodged something deep in the heart and soul of Walter, who stood up tall and extended his hand across the table. He said, "Walter Lee Johnson, Private First Class. Pleased to make your 'quaintance, sir."

Mary Elizabeth was not so charitably disposed toward the self-avowed Adversary of God and tried to stop her old friend. "Dub, no! You can't . . ."

"Ever'body need a friend, Mully. You been my friend for I don't know how long, when I was in a bad time. This poor fool say he ain't never had no friends. That ain't right. You know that ain't right." He was still offering his hand to Satan, who eyed it suspiciously. He looked at the Old Man, who nodded. "Your choice, Lucifer."

Satan, Archangel and eternal Adversary of the Lord God Almighty, Prince of Lies, the leader of the Heavenly Revolt, was, for the first time since leaving the heavenly realms, Not Sure.

Chapter 24

An Unlikely Thing to Speculate

Mickey Doyle, former US Army sergeant and retired beat cop, had only taken this job because Mr. Coleman the bank president had assured him that nothing ever happened at the Bank of Lawson. They'd never had any robbery attempts, disturbances of the peace, or even inordinate public displays of affection in the six years he'd worked there, or in the six decades before that. The last time a bank guard could have been useful was when a possum suspected of rabies had somehow gotten into the attic, but Mickey had been serving in Vietnam back then, where he'd seen all the action he'd ever wanted to see.

Now it looked like a young man with a Santa hat and beard was running right for him—Mickey couldn't be sure because his glasses were in his shirt pocket, and without his spectacles anything happening more than ten feet away from him was largely speculative. A skinny young Santa was an unlikely thing to speculate.

His left leg had fallen asleep, but he stood up as quickly as he could, unfolding his seventy-one-year-old bones and saying, "You're gonna have to get past me, punk!" in his best Clint Eastwood voice. Sometimes all you had to do was talk tough.

The kid didn't even slow down. He faked to the left and tried to get around Mickey to the right.

It almost worked; the kid almost got away untouched. But Mickey Doyle was surprisingly nimble for a septuagenarian. He partly lunged and partly fell, catching the panicky culprit around the waist. It was hard to believe such a scrawny kid could be so strong; there was almost nothing for the bank guard to grab on to. He kicked and squirmed until Mickey was having a hard time holding on to his thighs. The failed bank robber stepped on his hand, and as he freed the hand from under the kid's sneaker, his glasses fell out of his pocket and the skinny Santa stepped on them, too. Mickey roared, "Hold still, dammit!"

The kid was all feet and knees, all struggle and desperation. He pulled his right leg out of the guard's grasp, but Mickey caught his left in a stronger grip, determined that he would not fail. His wristwatch, the Bulova the Memphis Police Department had given him for twenty years of service, dug into the kid's ankle, peeling back a ribbon of skin until the blood gushed out. But the punk wriggled and lunged until all Mickey had was his shoe, and then the kid's foot pulled out of it, and he was gone. He bolted out the front door of the bank and ran off to the right, down Main.

Mickey's upper lip was bleeding; he could taste it. His glasses were smashed beyond repair. He was angry and embarrassed. He got up slowly and looked around at the vague shapes and colors inside the bank. Nobody seemed to be much concerned about him; they were already telling their stories about what had just happened, how it looked from where they'd been standing.

But there was something else. Mickey Doyle was also exhilarated. For the first time in years, his life had purpose. After the Army, after the Memphis Police Department, after his sweet Virginia had died on Christmas Eve four years ago, he hadn't had much to live for. Every Sunday he took their dog Barney to visit her grave; every week he told her that they were doing just fine, but he knew it was a lie. He was just going through the motions, just marching in place with nowhere left to go.

In all his years as an officer in the military and in the police, Mickey had never been so humiliated as he had just been at the hands—or feet—of this Santa bank robber. Now all he had to do was follow the trail of blood. The smile on his face was grim, but it was the first genuine smile he'd allowed himself in a long, long time.

Chapter 25

A Man Worthy of Respect

Vinnie and Carlos walked down the alley and looked to the left when they came to Buchanan Alley, the backstreet between Main and Jefferson. They didn't see anybody or anything. Vinnie pointed to the left and asked Carlos, "This way?"

"Sí, Boss."

They made their way down Buchanan, on the lookout for Santa or Tucker, mindful that the police were also likely to be out looking and knowing they wanted to avoid any interaction with Lawson's finest. When they came to Jefferson, they looked around a little, trying to imagine where the Santa might have gone.

"We lost him, Boss." Joey was out of breath, having hustled to keep up. "He ain't nowhere." He'd intended to say "He ain't nowhere to be found," but he'd run out of breath.

Vinnie snapped, "Nobody's nowhere, you idiot! Let's split up: I'll go this way"—he pointed to the right, away from the bank where the police car's lights were still flashing—"Carlos, you go that way—he pointed to the left, back toward the bank. Carlos knew better than to argue or complain, but he was not in any hurry to go that way, toward the law enforcement officials. Carlos nodded, and Vinnie continued, "Joey, you go back to the car and wait for us there."

"But Boss—"

Vinnie knew Joey hated to be left out, that he really wanted to help, and that he would do anything to please him. But Joey was too slow and too . . . conspicuous, too likely to draw unwanted attention. It would be easier to give Joey a task, something to make him feel included and important. He said, "Look, Joey. This Santa might make his way right past our car again. I mean, he was there once, right?" Joey nodded, and Vinnie continued. "So maybe he'll come back. And if he does, I need somebody strong enough to grab him and hold him until me and Carlos get back. It's important—can you do that?"

Joey beamed. "Yeah, Boss—you can count on me."

"I know, Joey—I always do.

Vinnie nodded to Carlos, and they went their different directions. Carlos walked slowly, cautiously, watching for the police who would be looking for anything suspicious, and thinking he was not in any hurry to come across a desperate and probably armed Santa who'd just robbed a bank.

In an alley off to his right he thought he heard a sound, like a woman singing. He knew he should keep going, but he was getting close enough to the blue lights of the police cars that his skin was starting to itch. As much as he loved his home country, he didn't want the *federales* to force him to go back. He had to be careful all the time, but . . . there was something about this song, something wise. It sounded like his grandmother, his *abuela*, singing to herself in the kitchen.

He ventured into the alley, listening for the woman. When he followed her song, he saw her sitting against the wall, leaning on a battered dumpster.

She was an old woman, with dark skin and hair that was mostly gray. She didn't look like most of the people he saw in the South, but he didn't think she was a Latina, either. She was wearing an old, worn dress, pale blue with white flowers, and the shawl over her shoulders was so faded he couldn't tell what color it might have been when it was new.

It was a surprise to see an old woman sitting in an alleyway, but the most surprising thing was that the air in this filthy alley smelled like roses.

Little Carlos asked, "Do you need some help, *abuela*?"

"No, *chico*—I am not the one who needs help."

"Who needs help? Is somebody helping you?"

"No, Carlos. You are the one in need."

"I don't know where you got that, but I'm okay. I'm just, um, trying to find a friend. He's wearing a Santa hat and beard, and he's missing one shoe. Have you seen him?"

"No, child. He is of no concern to you. Where are you going?"

"Like I said, I'm looking for a friend . . ."

"So Mr. Vinnie Carlisle and poor Joey Carolla can beat him and hurt him? Is that where you want to go?"

Carlos was deeply perturbed and perplexed by this conversation. He didn't know who this woman was or how she knew about Joey or Mr. C., but he wasn't sure he wanted to find out. There was clearly more to this lady than was apparent.

He said, "Look, lady—you need some money?" He reached for his wallet, remembering his life of poverty in Honduras, grateful that he had a five to give her. But she shook her head and said, "I do not need anything. It is yourself you should be concerned about."

Carlos looked at her again and saw her as if for the first time. There was something different about her, something odd about the way she looked. Actually, it wasn't that she herself looked unusual, but her surroundings seemed indistinct, almost dreamlike—as if the air around her was thick, somehow lingering around her. When he looked directly at her, the effect was most noticeable, but it was hard to look at her for long; when his eyes glanced away, she seemed clearer. And that unmistakable smell of roses was so clean, so wholesome, and so completely out of place in this dirty alley.

He was aware that his mouth was very dry; he had difficulty asking, "Who are you?"

"The question you should be asking is who are *you, mi amigo.*"

"I know who I am, *abuela.* I'm just doing a job here, and I've taken the time to see if you need help. I don't need riddles from an old bag lady, that's for sure!"

"No, Carlito, you are wrong. You no longer know who you are. You have lost yourself. You know that, deep in your heart; you know that you are not a man who would feel at ease hurting another man, a man you do not even know. Your mother taught you to be a man worthy of respect, not to be *el bandido.*"

He looked at her again. Something strange was happening here. Nobody called him Carlito except his mother. None of this made any sense. Knowing it was ridiculous even as he said it, he asked, "You know my mother?"

"*Sí*, Carlito. And your father, your brothers Jorge and Javier, and your *abuelo* Don Maximo who died on your way here to make a better life for his family. And you disgrace them, Carlito—you disgrace them by working with this Vinnie Carlisle."

"You know Mr. C., too?"

"Yes, of course."

"Who are you, *abuela*?"

"That is not what you need to know. The question you need to answer is the one I asked before: 'Where are you going?'"

"I . . . I don't know."

"No, you do not know. Thank you for being honest. I will tell you a story, a story you have heard before. This time may you hear it not only with your ears but also in your heart."

Carlo nodded, and the woman continued. "A man had two sons. The younger son wanted his inheritance from his father, who loved him and gave him half of everything he owned. The foolish son went away and bought everything he wanted and had women and friends and rich foods and drink, until he had spent all the money his father gave him. You know this story?"

"*Sí, abuela*—the story of the prodigal son."

"*Sí.* When the money was gone, the women and friends left with it, and the food and drink also. The foolish son had to find a job and worked for a man who kept pigs. He was lost, just as you are lost, *sí*?"

"*Sí.*"

She looked at him to see if he would hear the point of her telling the story, and when she was satisfied that he was listening, she continued. It was when she emphasized *"Y volviendo en sí"*—"When he came to himself"—that he realized they had been speaking in Spanish for several minutes. She was watching him intently, to see if he would catch the point of the story: "And when he came to himself, he knew that this was not who he was, that he should go back to his father and beg forgiveness. And when the foolish boy's father saw him coming, he threw a feast for him and gave him gifts, to celebrate his beloved son coming home."

Carlos's eyes were watering with tears he did not want. She was still looking at him closely, and it was unmanly to cry. He had to be strong, he had to be tough. "So?"

"So. It is time for you to come to yourself. This is not who you are, Carlito; this is not your path. It is time for you to decide who you are."

Chapter 26

Thou Art Just a Lie

Grayson Tucker's adrenaline was wearing off. He'd lost a shoe wrestling with the tough old bank guard. He still had the Santa hat and beard, but other than that all he had was panic and confusion.

Not only might he be caught by the police for attempted bank robbery, not only were Vinnie Carlisle and his goons coming to collect eight thousand dollars he still didn't have, not only was he in imminent danger of either going to jail or having his legs broken or his fingers cut off or something even worse that he really didn't want to contemplate, but now he'd gotten himself all turned around. He didn't know which of the back-alley doors would lead into Stardust Comics, where his friend Jeremy might be able to offer the only help that was even remotely possible, or at least give him a place to hide.

He had taken a right out of the bank, run down Main Street until he could make it to the alley between the bank and the post office, taken the alley between the sandwich shop and the accountants' office, doubled back on Jefferson, cut back between the pawn shop and the ham radio store, and headed right on the backstreet between Jefferson and Main. Somewhere in all that, he'd run right past Mr. C.'s big goon Joey, and now all he could do was keep going. All the shops looked the same from the back, and he was lost.

He stopped running and stood panting for a minute or so, his hands on his knees. He was wheezing so loudly he was afraid the police would hear him. He tried to slow his breathing or at least make it a little less audible. His shoeless foot had a long cut from his ankle halfway up his calf, which was bleeding furiously.

He thought he knew his way around the backstreets behind Jefferson, but nothing looked familiar. The back doors of the various shops and stores all looked alike—no numbers, no way to find out which was which except to go around to the front of the store. He considered taking one of the little alleyways back to Main Street to find out where he was, but it would come with the huge risk of being seen, either by the cops or by Carlisle or one of his goons. It would be safer to open one of the doors and find out which shop he was behind.

But surely the shopkeepers had been paying attention to all the blue lights flashing at the bank building. What if somebody in the shop recognized him and called the police? What if Carlisle or that big brute Joey happened to be in there, avoiding the cops or looking for him?

No, he thought, better to find a place to hide here on the backstreet. He looked around and saw a dark spot between an HVAC unit and some garbage cans. He walked over, and before he could look too closely he forced himself to sit down on the cold, hard, stinking ground. He pulled one of the garbage cans in front of him so he couldn't easily be seen. Now he just had to wait until things blew over.

His ankle was starting to hurt, and he looked at it now. Not only had he lost his shoe, but the long cut looked pretty serious. He peered up into the slice of the sky he could see between the buildings and saw that it was getting cloudy. "Aw, man—c'mon!" he whispered to himself. "What else could go wrong?" Then he looked around and laughed humorlessly. "Who the hell you talking to, man?"

Then a wild idea came to him: he could pray. He didn't believe any of that stuff, but he thought "What the hell?" He didn't have any place to go or anything to do, and it probably couldn't hurt anything.

"Um, hello?" he whispered. "Jesus, or God? Anybody there?"

He wasn't off to an inspiring start. He tried again: "Our Father, who art in heaven—hollowed be thy name."

No, that can't be right; surely God's name is not hollowed? Now he felt a more familiar sensation, the terror of every actor who's ever been on the stage: he couldn't remember his lines! Maybe the most importance performance of his life, and he couldn't remember . . .

Then another wild idea hit him. This was not a performance at all; it had to be a genuine conversation, or it was a complete waste of time. Either way, he was going to give it a try, and try to do it right.

"Good Lord, it is thy servant Tucker. Grayson, I mean. Thou knowest me, and I know Thee very little, or not at all. I art sorry I hast not prayed much in all my life and have mostly ignored Thee. But now I need Thy help, see, and . . ."

He heard a car coming toward him, rolling down the backstreet; a police cruiser passed by slowly. Tucker put his head between his knees and didn't look up. He counted a hundred thumping heartbeats and didn't hear anything.

He prayed, "Look, Lord, I'm sorry. If You could just get me out of this, I'll . . . I'll do better—I promise."

Nothing happened.

"Get me out of trouble just this once, help me out, and I'll go to church and everything, all right?"

Still nothing happened. Tucker waited several minutes. He was cold, his foot was bleeding, and he had to pee. How long would he have to wait for divine intervention? If God was going to do something, Tucker wished He would hurry it up.

He sat for a while, trying not to move, listening for somebody looking for him. He whispered, "God?"

There was no answer.

"God—look, man: I really need you, all right?"

There was no answer.

"God—God *damn* it! I knew you weren't up there all along! You're just a lie!"

He was getting sleepy, and his ankle was aching. He knew he ought to do something to stop the bleeding, but he didn't have anything clean to press against it. He felt weak, and he was thirsty, and his head still hurt from way too much tequila the night before. He was cold, and the ground was hard, and the garbage stank. He wasn't thinking straight or seeing clearly. He wished his mama would come and find him. He wished God would . . . no. He whispered, "I've given up on you, God. Thou art just a lie."

And then, just before he fell asleep, he thought he heard a full rich harmony of voices saying, "Then who art thou talking to?"

Chapter 27

An Unheard but Decidedly Unhappy Song

The Rev. Thomas James McBride came into the presence of the Lord God Almighty in a most unexpected fashion: he walked into Fuddy's Pie Emporium on a Friday afternoon with a heretical or at least lapsed Roman Catholic attorney and slow-pitch shortstop. The little bell rang when he opened the door, just as it always had, but as soon as he walked into the place, it seemed clear that something had changed.

Narni wasn't behind the counter, for one thing; she was sitting in the far back corner with those two homeless people that came around sometimes and two men Mac had never seen before. His first thought was that the older one would make a good Santa. It was the beard and hair, maybe, but there was something else about him, something friendly, something familiar. He thought he would remember if he'd ever met anybody like that, but—well, maybe he was somebody Mac had always wanted to meet.

The other man gave Mac the creeps, like a grasping divorce court lawyer or maybe a slick television evangelist. He was leaning over, listening intently as the older man spoke. Mac was surprised by how much he wanted to hear what the bearded man was saying, too.

Mrs. Ralph Ketchum was at the counter, her lips pursed, her foot tapping a rhythm to an unheard but decidedly unhappy song. She cleared her throat to announce that she was waiting impatiently. Nobody else chose to notice, so Mac tried to help.

"Mrs. Ketchum?"

She turned around and seemed disappointed that it was Mac. She said, "Oh, Father McBride. Maybe you can get the girl's attention. I've been standing here for half an hour!"

"Well, I'm pretty sure I was talking to you in front of the post office about ten minutes ago."

"Well, I never! I'm sure I have better things to do than stand here and be insulted by a priest!"

"I meant no offense, ma'am. Let me see if I can catch Narni's eye."

Mac walked toward the back of the Emporium and was trying to think of what to say when the Old Man looked at him—*into* him—and said, "Thomas, Narni is in the middle of something here. Could you help Mrs. Ketchum? She just wants a pie; you can find them in the cooler in the back."

Mac felt his body moving away from the little table at the back of the shop, even as his mind and heart screamed that he wanted to stay there. He asked the Old Man, "What kind of pie does she want?" Then he had to admit at least to himself that he already knew the answer to the question, and that all he really wanted was to hear the Old Man say something, anything. There was something about his voice . . .

The Old Man smiled, and everything seemed like it was going to be all right. He said, "Lemon icebox. You can put it on my tab. Thank you, Thomas."

Mac was stunned by the luxurious vibrancy of the man's voice. He realized that, more than anything else in the world, he wanted to do what the man had asked him to do. He turned away somewhat reluctantly and then stopped. "After I give her the pie, can I come back?"

Then Fuddy's World Famous Pie Emporium was filled with the Old Man's laughter, and Mac's heart soared. "Yes, of course you can." Mac was looking for a pie in the cooler in the back before he realized that the Old Man had called him Thomas—not Father, not Mac. No one had called him Thomas since his mother died. He felt a chill and knew it was not because he was standing in front of the cooler.

He walked back to the counter with the lemon icebox pie. He said, "Here you go, Mrs. Ketchum."

"What is that?"

"It's the lemon icebox pie you came for." Mac paused, and then continued, "That's what you wanted, right?"

Mrs. Ralph Ketchum was indignant. It was what she did best; she'd been indignant for so long about so many things that it was altogether likely she'd gotten stuck in it. Indignation had become the background music of her life.

She said, making sure she spoke loudly enough for everyone in the Emporium to hear, "Who told you I wanted a lemon icebox pie?"

Mac pointed to the man sitting at the table in the back and said, "He did."

"And how am I to pay for it if the young woman refuses to come and do her job?"

"He said to put in on his tab."

"And who gave him the idea that he could speak for me or pay for my pie?"

But Mac was weary of Mrs. Ketchum and had already turned to walk away. He didn't know what they were talking about back there, only that he wanted to hear the man speak again, about anything.

Mrs. Ketchum looked at Early Miller, who had no idea what was going on. It was not unfamiliar territory for Early; he shrugged and followed his friend Mac to the back corner.

Mrs. Ralph Ketchum was not accustomed to being ignored or having a stranger buy something for her, and she was not going to stand for it. When things were in their proper order, workers in shops and restaurants should get what she told them to get, people she encountered on the streets should listen to what she had to say and move along, and people she did not know were strangers and there-fore undeserving of her attention. In her view of the world, this is how it had been for decades and how it should always be. The very idea of letting the pie shop girl neglect her duties, of being handed a pie by the liberal priest who then shrugs and walks away, of having a complete stranger buy her a pie—this was not to be tolerated.

In an unsolicited moment of clarity, she caught a glimpse of a disturbing idea—perhaps the world about her was not about her at all. But . . . no. "Well, we'll see about that!" she announced to the walls of the Pie Emporium. She gathered steam as she set her course for the back of the shop. Stopping six or seven feet short of the table, she cleared her throat again. Nobody noticed her, and her voice was somewhat shrill when she spoke. "Young woman! Are you working at all today?"

Narni started to stand up, but the Old Man stopped her with a gentle hand on her shoulder. He addressed Mrs. Ralph Ketchum with a nod of his head and a twinkle in his eyes: "Good afternoon, Millie. It is so good to see you."

Chapter 28

Spinning Out of Control

Mac was astounded, intrigued, dumbfounded. He pulled up a chair and sat beside Narni, and Early sat beside him. It turns out the old battleship had a first name after all—Millie!

It was difficult for Mrs. Ralph Ketchum to see through all that indignation with which she armored herself, and harder still to understand how anyone could have pierced it. For most of her adult life, her imperious attitude had been more than enough to keep people at the distance she preferred, out of her way but eager to do her bidding. And this man—this stranger, this outsider—had the temerity to call her Millie? Everyone in this town spoke to her with the esteem she felt she deserved, with the sort of respectful decorum she had worked her whole life to achieve. But this man . . .

"Pardon me, sir, it seems you are under the impression that you know me."

He chuckled. (Mrs. Ralph Ketchum was chagrined—he'd actually laughed at her!) She was just about to set him straight, tell him who she was, had taken the breath to deliver her salvo, when he said, "Yes, child, I know you. I know who you are and who you were. It was not so long ago that you were Mildred Louise McMahon, growing up with your sisters in that little house on Pine Street. Do you remember?"

"No! You . . . you can't talk to me like—you can't know—you . . . Just who do you think you are, sir?"

"Would you like to join us, Millie?"

"I would like to be treated with the respect I deserve, sir."

"You need to be careful about that, Millie."

"About what?"

"About asking to be treated as you deserve to be treated."

"Well, I never!"

Mary Elizabeth snapped, "Well, maybe you should start now!"

Mrs. Ralph Ketchum gave no indication of having heard Mary Elizabeth. She was not accustomed to being afraid, but this man scared her. She folded her arms in front of her abundant bosom and said, still looking at the Old Man, "Sir, I demand to know who you are!"

This caused something of an uproar at the table, with everyone responding in her or his own way, all of them at once:

Mac—"Mrs. Ketchum, please!"

Narni—"You can't talk to Him like that!"

Satan—"Sir, must we endure this odious creature?"

Walter—"Jus' sit down and shut up."

Mary Elizabeth—"Best you jus' keep your quiet, Miss High and Mighty!"

Early—"Hooboy!"

Only the Old Man was quiet; He sat serenely, His smile unfading, unfazed. But everyone else in Fuddy's was staggered:

Mac at the volume and vehemence of condemnation directed at Mrs. Ketchum;

Narni at Mrs. Ketchum's reaction to having several people stand up to her at once;

Satan at finding any sort of common cause with the humans;

Walter at himself for talking to a white woman that way;

Mary Elizabeth at how free she suddenly was to speak her mind;

Early at how much fun the afternoon was turning out to be;

And Mrs. Ralph Ketchum, now revealed as Millie, at being spoken to in this way. She whispered to herself again: "Well, I . . . never."

The Old Man, still untroubled, repeated, "Would you like to join us, Millie?"

Walter pulled up a chair and gestured for her to be seated with the graceful flourish of a magician, the *voilà* unspoken but implied.

It was not her understanding of the world that she should be told what to do, that a street person should offer her a chair, or that anyone should call her by her Christian name. She felt woozy, the coffee shop seeming to spin out of control. She sat in the chair the homeless man had offered her, somewhat more heavily than she would have thought proper.

"Now, Ben, my friend Walter has extended his hand to you, knowing full well who you are, to invite your friendship. What will you do?"

Everyone looked at Satan, even Millie Ketchum, as she followed the others' eyes. The younger stranger closed his eyes and exhaled. "I was hoping you would forget about that."

When the Old Man laughed, all the others laughed with him, except for Satan and Millie, who felt an urge to laugh, not because she understood why the others were laughing but because of the sheer joy she felt in the moment, but she repressed it. It would have been . . . unseemly. An unwelcome thought barged into her mind, and she tried unsuccessfully to remember the last time she'd actually laughed. She thought of herself as a keen observer of human nature, but she had never heard anyone laugh like this man, with so little restraint. And his voice . . .

"As you surely know, I do not forget. What will you do?"

"My Lord, I . . . don't think I can."

"Of course you can. It may be that you will not. For you, for all of you, it is always a matter of what you will and what you will not. What you choose determines who you are."

Mrs. Ralph Ketchum had used the moment to recover herself. She put her hand on Mac's arm and whispered, "Father Mac, who are these people?"

Mac clearly didn't want her to interrupt what was being said, but he leaned over and whispered, "I'm not sure. I mean, I know Narni, and I've seen, um, Mary Elizabeth and Walter around. Early you may know, but these other two, I . . . I just don't know."

"Well, I don't like them. I wish they would go back to wherever they belong."

"Oh, I don't know. I'm just . . ."

But just what the Rev. Thomas McBride was at that moment, Millie Ketchum would not know, because just then the shop bell announced the arrival of Vinnie Carlisle, aspiring mob boss.

Only the Old Man seemed to notice his entrance. He nodded His satisfaction and smiled peacefully. "Narni, my dear," He said, "will you offer our new guest a cup of coffee and some of that marvelous pie, please? I Am sure he soon will be joining us as well."

Narni stood and went to the counter, only half-aware of the movement behind her as Walter pulled up another chair. Millie Ketchum and the Old Man didn't move, He sitting serenely and she in great agitation. When the newcomer stepped toward the cluster of tables, the grandfatherly figure said, "It is good to see you. Please come and join us."

Vinnie sized up the situation quickly and decided to use his reliable tactic of going on the offensive. He said, "Who the hell are you, pal?"

Vinnie was gratified at the titter around the tables, as he believed his aggressive question would establish him as the attacker and put the Old Man on the defensive; it was exactly how Vinnie liked to work. But the Old Man kept His tranquil smile as He answered, "I Am glad you think of me as your pal."

Vinnie was stunned, speechless. The Old Man repeated His invitation, "Please come and join us," and added, "Would you like some world famous lemon icebox pie?"

Vinnie was clearly bewildered, but he sat down cautiously, and they spent a moment in silent anticipation until Satan, who seemed much more comfortable with this new member of their circle, declared, "So, Danny Royce Elkins. I have so been looking forward to seeing you."

Chapter 29

Looking for Blood

Mickey Doyle was on the case. Let all the young cops with their expensive equipment huddle behind their cruiser doors; let them check their precious computers for information. Doyle was following the trail of blood, which would lead him right to the perpetrator.

The police had interviewed him, asked him to describe the suspect: "young, skinny, medium height, wearing a Santa hat and beard, missing left shoe." No, he hadn't seen any gang marks or tattoos. No, the perp hadn't said anything; no, he couldn't tell them anything else.

The young lieutenant had gotten in his face, talking to him like he was stupid, bullying him for more information. He demanded that Mickey hand over his service revolver and gave it a hard look for no reason at all before giving it back like he was doing him a favor, and Mickey decided he didn't have to tell Lt. Pimpleface anything, not even that the guy had turned to the right coming out of the bank. The clown didn't even ask which way the guy had run. Serves him right. Let him figure it out.

When he was released from their interrogation, Mickey went to his car to get his old pair of scratched-up glasses. He worried that the trail would be cold, but he found small drops of blood as he went down Main Street in the direction the Santa had taken. He thought he'd lost him for a minute or two, but then he thought, "What would I do? I sure as hell wouldn't be running down Main Street with the cops looking for me. I'd be taking one of the backstreets, like the alley that runs between Main and Jefferson." Mickey ducked between the barbershop and the Flower Power Gift Shoppe and found several drops of blood on the concrete outside the barber's—he was still on the trail. He turned down the backstreet, looking both ways for Santa One Shoe.

He scanned the pavement, searching for drops of telltale blood. He didn't have as much light as he would have liked, and his eyes weren't what they used to be, especially wearing these old glasses, but he wasn't about to go back to his car to get his flashlight, not when the little creep could be making a clean escape.

He didn't see any more blood, and worried for a moment that the kid was going to get away, at least from him. He decided if he was running, he'd be running away from the bank where the cops were—he'd be heading west toward the park, past that place with the good pie and the funnybook store.

He turned to his left, still searching for blood on the ground. He didn't see anything, just some garbage cans, a stack of old cardboard boxes flattened out, an air conditioner unit. A few steps more took him behind Gary's Gizmos and Gadgets, which had filled the small vacuum for ham radio and stereo enthusiasts when the Radio Shack had gone out of business.

He took a few more careful steps, and then he saw it: blood on the pavement, lots of it, everywhere. He tried to read a pattern, get some sense of direction, but there was too much. Then he saw what he thought would crack the case of Santa One Shoe: blood on the handle on the door to the funnybook shop—a red drop running down the gray metal door.

In the excitement of the chase, Mickey Doyle was looking for blood. He wasn't looking for red paint, so he hadn't seen it at first.

He tried the door; it wasn't locked. He could go back for the police and let them do their job. But the little creep had kicked him in the face and broken his glasses; this was personal. "And anyways," he whispered to himself, "I ain't goin' back to Lieutenant Snotnose if I ain't sure Santa's holed up in here."

He took a deep breath, opened the door, and walked in behind his gun, his finger on the trigger.

Chapter 30

Twenty-Seven Green M&M's

Jeremy was having a slow day at Stardust Comics, another in a long line of slow days. He'd tried to call Narni so many times he'd lost count; he was worried that he'd burned his last and best bridge. He loved her so much; he'd tried so hard to make her happy, but . . .

He just couldn't. She wasn't going to be happy as long as she was with him. She wasn't going to be happy in Lawson. She'd told him she was sick of him, sick of Lawson, and sick of world famous lemon icebox pie. She'd said it was okay for him: he was a small-town guy. She'd said that she wanted to be a big-city woman. He said he'd come with her, find a job in New York while she was writing and trying to break into the comics business, but she said no. "It's not that I don't want to be with you—I just don't want you to be unhappy. You'd be miserable in New York, Jeremy."

And that's when he'd snapped. "Goddamn it, Narni! You'll never make it in New York, either. You'll never make it writing comic books. This isn't your dream—it's a fantasy! The difference between you and me is that I've accepted who I am, and you're . . . you're just chasing illusions!"

He hadn't meant to say any of that; he hadn't meant to hurt her. It wasn't even what he believed—after he'd said it, he'd wondered where it came from. He was just hurt and frustrated and afraid and . . . childish and petty and mean. But now it was too late; he couldn't take it back; he couldn't unsay it. And now she wasn't answering her cellphone. He thought about walking down to Fuddy's but decided against it. He told himself it was because he didn't want to put her on the spot, but he knew the truth was that he was scared: afraid of the reception he might find there, afraid she would tell him it was over.

One of the Christmas parties at the Hound Dog the night before had left a table full of snacks and appetizers largely untouched.

Jeremy had seen it before the cooks and wait staff, and he'd loaded up his pockets with peanut M&M's.

Jeremy had loved M&M's since the eighth grade, when he and Grady Kilgore had tried to start their own superstition by telling their classmates that you had to eat the green M&M's last, or it would rain. And you had to eat all the green M&M's at the same time. Nobody had paid them any attention, the superstition had failed, and Jeremy had long since lost touch with Grady Kilgore. But it made him feel good to eat the green M&M's last, so he did. If it rained, it wasn't going to be his fault.

At Stardust Comics that morning, he's put all the purloined M&M's on the counter, separating them into their tribes: yellow, orange, brown, red, blue, and lastly, green. It was something to do, and he was desperate for something to do. He'd been eating them all morning, and now he was down to the green ones—twenty-seven green peanut M&M's.

Nobody was in the store; nobody had been in all day. He took a deep breath and put all the green peanut M&M's in his mouth. He was relishing the sheer silliness of it the moment a crazy man wearing a uniform and holding a gun suddenly burst through the back door.

"Hands in the air!" he yelled. "Don't say a word!"

Jeremy froze, unable to tell the crazy man he couldn't have said anything if he wanted to with his mouth full of M&M's.

The man yelled again: "Hands in the air, punk!"

Jeremy put his hands in the air and considered spitting out all the M&M's, but he decided to chew them up instead. Later, he wondered if that might have been a mistake.

Doyle looked at the young man and saw that he was chewing frantically. He knew what that meant—he was eating a bag of pot or some other illicit substance he didn't want to be caught with. He also noticed that the perpetrator looked like he was scared to death. "What's your name, kid?" The young man behind the counter just looked at him, still chewing. He repeated himself, this time more forcefully: "What's your damn name?"

Jeremy tried to say his name, but he had a mouthful of partially chewed green peanut M&M's, so it sounded more like "Cherchermle" with a choking cough somewhere in the middle.

Mickey Doyle had seen a lot of things in the jungles of Vietnam and on the streets of Memphis, many of them things he never wanted to see or think about again. But he had never seen anybody's mouth foaming with some kind of green chunky excretion. It was spluttering out of the kid's mouth, down his chin, and onto his shirt. "This kid's on some kind of drugs," thought Mickey, "and that makes him dangerous." Mickey hated drugs; he'd seen too much of that stuff, too.

"Down on the floor!" he ordered. The young man lowered one hand but held up the other, chewed for a few seconds, swallowed, and lay down without a word.

"All right, Santa—where's your gun?" If the guy was robbing the bank, surely he'd had a gun.

"I don't have a gun!" Jeremy yelled with his nose pressed to the floor. Now that he had cleared his mouth of M&M's, he was trying to figure out why an armed man was robbing the comic book store. Maybe the man thought he had a gun under the counter to protect the cash register or something. But why had he called him Santa?

"Where's your goddamn gun?"

"I don't have one!"

"Where'd you put it?"

"There is no gun!"

Mickey looked down and saw that the kid had both shoes on. He could have put on a new pair of shoes, but it seemed unlikely, and these certainly didn't look new. More likely this was not the guy who'd tried to rob the bank. Just a kid doing some kind of weird new street drug. But the trail of blood drops had led into this store; maybe this guy knew the perp; maybe he was hiding him or knew where he was or where he would be going.

"All right, stand up. You're going to jail, kid, so you might as well tell me the truth."

Jeremy lay on the floor, trying to get a grip on what was happening. The man with the gun was the police. Surely he wouldn't be taken to jail for excessive M&M consumption—twenty-seven wasn't even his record. None of it made any sense until the man continued, "Where's your friend with the Santa beard and hat?"

Tucker. In a soul-freezing moment of clarity, Jeremy knew that the man with a gun was looking for Tucker, and he was going to take Jeremy to jail for aiding and abetting a counterfeit Santa Claus in the act of defrauding the guilt-ridden.

Jeremy wondered what kind of trouble Tucker had gotten himself into this time. He turned his head as he got up from the floor and saw one more M&M: one last green one. Apparently it had fallen earlier. It was a crazy thought, but it was sort of a crazy moment, and it fit right in: for the first time since the eighth grade, he hadn't eaten all the green M&M's together, and just look what happened. Surely it would rain this afternoon, he thought.

He took his time standing up, trying to clear his head, coming to grips with his situation. There was a lot Jeremy didn't know, but he was absolutely sure about one thing: he was looking at a man who had a pistol pointed at him. He thought fleetingly about protecting his friend Tucker, but it didn't last. The man had a pistol and was clearly deranged. His hands still in the air, he said as casually as he could, "You're looking for Tucker. He had the Santa hat and beard."

"Tucker who?"

"No, Tucker's his last name. It's, um, Grayson. Grayson Tucker."

"Friend of yours?"

"Sort of."

"Drug buddy?"

"What? Well, some pot, mostly years ago. I've haven't had any for three or four weeks now. My girlfriend—well, my former girl-friend—told me—"

"Shut up."

"Yes, sir."

"Where is this Grayson Tucker now?"

"I don't know, sir. If you don't mind telling me, why are you looking for him?"

"I'm asking the questions here, punk."

"What did he do?"

"Tried to rob the Bank of Lawson. Probably getting enough money to buy whatever drug you're on."

"I'm not on any drug!"

"What's all that green stuff coming out of your mouth, then?"

"Peanut M&M's, sir." Jeremy was regaining his composure a little and tried to say it with as much dignity as he could, which was a challenge. He leaned down to pick up the escaped twenty-seventh to display the evidence: "Twenty-six green peanut M&M's."

Chapter 31

Will You Lie to Yourself?

Joey was still waiting by the car, all by himself. The little Santa guy had not come back, he hadn't encountered any police, and Little Carlos and Mr. C. were nowhere to be seen. He was alone, and he never liked that. He wondered how long they'd been gone and when they'd come back. He wondered if they'd ever find this guy Tucker now that he was on the run from the police, too. He wondered when they were going to have something to eat—it had been a long time since their barbecue lunch.

"Hey, Joey!" It was Little Carlos, trotting toward him. "You seen Mr. C.?"

"No, I ain't seen him or anybody else. It's just me and the car."

"Okay, great. Listen, Joey: I'm out of here, all right?"

"What do you mean, out of here? What's that mean?"

"It means I'm taking off. Look, here are the keys to the Mercedes. Just give them to Mr. C. and tell him I went back to Honduras."

"You goin' back to Honduras?"

"Yeah, tell him I'm going back to Honduras."

"Did something happen?"

"Yeah. I think I might'a had a vision or something, man."

"What do you mean, a vision? What's that mean?"

"I think it was the Virgin of Suyapa, man!"

"It was what?"

"The Virgin Mary, you know the Virgin Mary?"

"Yeah?"

"In Honduras, we call her the Virgin of Suyapa because of a little statue of her in a shrine in Suyapa, a town outside of Tegucigalpa."

Joey looked effortlessly unimpressed.

"The thing is, the Virgin Mary's like a big deal in Honduras, see? And I think I just talked to her!"

Now Joey was round-eyed and filled with wonder. "What did she say?"

"She said, "When he came to himself . . .'"

"What does that mean?"

"It means this is not who I am."

"Who are you, then?"

"I am a man. I want to do what is right from now on."

"So you're leaving?"

"Yeah, man—I'm leaving."

"But you're leaving me with the keys to the car? You coulda just stole it, man."

"Yeah, I thought about that. I've gotten pretty good at stealing cars, you know? But that's not something I want to be good at. I want to be proud of who I am. I'm not stealing anything anymore, man—never again."

Little Carlos Pineda handed over the keys to the Mercedes with his left hand and held out his right hand to shake Joey's hand. They weren't friends, but they were colleagues, and Carlos wanted to part with him honorably. Joey shook his hand and marveled at the change in him. Carlos turned and started to walk away, saying, "*Adios, amigo.*"

Joey watched him walk a few steps and then asked one last question: "Where did you say you saw this Virgin Mary Sue somethin'?" Carlos pointed back toward the Bank of Lawson and said, "About a hundred feet that way. Just past the comic book store, to the right."

Joey watched Little Carlos until he turned the corner, and then he was gone. Joey didn't believe in ghosts or spirits, and he didn't believe Little Carlos had seen the Virgin Mary. But it sure seemed like the guy had seen something past the funnybook store to the right.

It was a little bit of a struggle, but Joey convinced himself that Mr. C. would want him to look into whatever Little Carlos had seen or heard, so he wandered that way. It didn't take him long to find a woman in the alley; she was right where Carlos had said she'd be. But she didn't look like anything miraculous or life-changing to Joey— just a faded old woman down on her luck.

He said, "Hey."

She looked at him with a sorrow he did not notice and answered, "Joseph."

"It's just Joey."

"He was the love of my life, you know: Joseph."

"Who?"

"My husband. A good man. Are you a good man, Joseph?"

"Well . . . no'm, I don't think so. You can't be a good man and do what I do."

"Then you should do something else."

"It ain't that easy. I can't just—"

"Of course you can. You simply do not want to."

This infuriated Joey. "What the hell do you know about it? You're just an old bag lady or somethin'."

She sighed and stood, much more gracefully than Joey would have thought possible. He wondered how old she was but couldn't tell. Her eyes never left his, and he found he couldn't look away from those dark eyes, full of love and sadness. But there was something more in her eyes: he saw his mother's eyes, and he wished he could have done better, been better. She said, "I have known men like you before, men who hide behind the orders they are given and take no responsibility for what they do. It is easier that way, I think: just do what Vinnie Carlisle tells you to do—nothing is ever your fault, you never have to decide. Just do what Mr. C. tells you to do."

"How do you know Mr. C.?"

She looked at him with sincere pity, and he continued, "And what did you do to Carlos?"

"I just helped him remember who he is. There is more to him than just doing whatever another tells him to do. But you . . ."

"Yeah? What about me, old lady?"

"I am afraid there may be nothing more to you. If you continue along the path you are walking, I think you will continue to take another man's orders until you are killed. Not for love or loyalty, but for money. It is a shameful life, Joseph Carolla. You know that it is."

Joey was stunned by the old woman and hurt by her words. "You don't know anything! You're just an old tramp, or a gypsy or somethin'! I ain't scared of you!"

"No, Joseph. It is not I you need fear. I will not hurt you. I will just tell you the truth. Do you want to know the truth?"

Joey hesitated. Something about this raggedy old woman caught at his long-ignored imagination, something he wanted to hear more about. But despite his bluster, he was afraid. "Go to hell, bitch! I ain't scared of you!"

"Very well," she said, as calm as the minute before dawn. "Then I will be on my way." She turned and started to walk down the alley, away from Joey, who was still struggling with his thoughts. He knew he was missing out on something, but he didn't know what. She was almost to the corner, and she would be gone soon.

Joey ran after her. "Hey, wait up!"

She turned to face him, and it seemed to Joey that she was taller than she had been, more formidable.

"Okay, he said. "What do you want to tell me?"

"I do not want to tell you anything, Joseph. What do you want to know?"

"You said you could tell me the truth."

"I asked if you wanted to know the truth."

"Yeah, okay. Tell me the truth."

She crossed her arms and looked at him sternly. "The truth is that your mother still loves you and misses you. She prays for you every day."

"What? My mother—you don't know anything about . . ."

"Your mother, Clydean Pearce Carolla, married your father Charlie when she was just sixteen years old. She became a Roman Catholic soon after that, and because of that, she never saw her own mother again. She lights a candle for you every year on your birthday."

"No! That ain't true! You're just makin' all that stuff up!"

"Your mother's name is not Clydean? She didn't marry your father when she was sixteen? You know those things are true, Joseph. To protect yourself from the truth, will you lie to yourself?"

"You . . . you put some kind of spell on me. You're a witch or somethin'."

"No, I am telling you the truth. Your mother loves you. You should go home."

"I can't . . . I can't just—"

"Of course you can, Joseph."

"But what about Mr. C.?"

"Vinnie Carlisle is not your concern, Joseph. It is time for you to look after yourself. Go home. Be loved."

Then she turned and walked away, leaving Joey Carolla to wonder if she was the wisest person he'd ever met or just another crazy street lady.

Chapter 32

The Most Interesting Friday Afternoon Ever

Earl Bloom Miller, Esquire, couldn't remember when he'd had so much fun, certainly not since his fraternity days in college. Law school and a failed marriage had not been remotely fun, and his law practice made watching rocks erode look exciting by comparison. He had no idea what was going on at Fuddy's this afternoon, but that was fine with him—in fact, having no idea was the way he preferred it.

He'd been named after his Uncle Earl, a successful attorney in Birmingham, which is also where he'd inherited his vocation—his mother would have it no other way. Her son was going to follow his uncle's path through life, which meant he was going to be an attorney, and there was never any reason to have a discussion about it.

Bloom was his mother's maiden name, and it also explained why his mother was named Rose and her sisters were Lily, Daisy, and Petunia. It was, as his grandmother had proudly and repeatedly pointed out, a theme.

His father's name was Tommy Miller, and he was apparently very attractive and completely worthless. He'd been a star baseball pitcher in high school and had some scholarship offers, but he left the day after his cheerleader girlfriend told him she was pregnant, and they'd never heard from him again.

When little Earl was born three weeks premature, one aunt had called him Early, and the name stuck. Another aunt had wistfully whispered she'd been hoping it was going to be a girl; they could have called her Violet.

Uncle Earl had stepped in, providing a small house on the outskirts of Lawson and serving as his orphan nephew's guardian and protector. When Early graduated from high school, he told his mother and his uncle that he wanted to go to Delta State to play baseball and study history. He was informed that he would be going to Ole Miss and that he would major in Political Science on his way to law school.

Early had been baptized as an infant at Our Lady of the Immaculate Conception there in Lawson, had taken his first Communion when he was seven, and had been confirmed when he was eleven. After he'd passed the bar and his mother had moved to Birmingham to take care of her brother Earl, he moved back into the old family home next to his maiden aunts Daisy and Petunia, and he stopped going to church. He told the concerned priest that he'd had enough confessions, homilies, stale Styrofoam-like bread, and sugary-sweet wine to last him the rest of his life.

He'd married an Ole Miss sorority girl who was convinced that he could be so much more, and four years later he'd signed the divorce papers because they'd both had to admit that he was all he was ever going to be. They'd tried to have children but were glad they hadn't when it came time to sign the papers.

He'd met Father Mac when the assistant district attorney, a Christmas and Easter member of St. Paul's, had invited him to come to a practice for his church league softball team. He'd been assured that he wouldn't have to join the church or even come to services, and the assistant DA promised that he would like their minister. The thing that impressed him the most that first evening was not that they had two coolers of beer at their practice but that he had to ask his friend which one was the preacher.

When the practice was over—mostly taking turns hitting fly balls and trying to work out how to execute a double play—a short stack of pizzas arrived "to wash down the beer." In the ensuing collegial banter, Early Miller was revealed as somebody who actually knew how to play baseball and instantly became not only their shortstop but also their player-coach. And just like that, for the first time since his wild days in college, he was part of a community. It was good to belong.

And for maybe the first time ever, he felt like he could be who he was instead of who somebody else wanted him to be.

He liked Mac. He liked the guys on the softball team. They weren't much good at softball, but they didn't seem to mind losing, and they had a lot of fun, win or lose. They especially liked playing the Lutheran team—the Wittenberg Warriors—because the Lutherans usually didn't have enough players to field a team, so some of the Episcopal team—the Via Media—switched over to fill their empty spots. Neither team cared who won, and it was good for everybody to have a chance to play.

St. Paul's Episcopal Church was also the first team in the church softball league to have a woman play. It had been an unwritten rule that it was a men's activity, but Trudie Svoboda, a dental hygienist recently returned to the area, had played college softball for the Millsaps Majors, and she asked Mac if she could join the team. Mild-mannered liberal that he was, he'd told her she could and that they would face together whatever pushback came their way. If any of the opposing teams had issues with it, they kept it quiet, not wanting to reveal themselves as the sexist chauvinists they were raised to be.

Trudie had grown up going to the big non-denominational megachurch outside of Tupelo and married her Episcopal boyfriend a few months after they graduated from college. She moved back home to Lawson after what sounded like a messy divorce; she told Early that her husband was like a dog that ran after cars—"He couldn't help chasing women, but he never knew what to do when he caught one." She told Mac that in the divorce, "He got the house, but I got the church. I never really liked that house, anyway."

Early adored her but kept his feelings to himself, not wanting to move too quickly. He did change dentists, though, thinking it might be nice to look forward to having his teeth cleaned. And Trudie made softball practice a whole lot more fun.

If you asked him, Early Miller would have told you that he only had one skill, and that was reading people. He wouldn't have said he was never wrong in this, but he believed he was usually right; it was something he took some pride in. He had been trying to get a handle on the group of people at Fuddy's that afternoon. He knew Mac, of course, and Narni, and he'd seen the two homeless people around town and given them a few dollars from time to time. Everybody knew Mrs. Ralph Ketchum, and he'd learned years ago that the only thing he wanted to get from her was away. But the Old Man and his younger and more sinister companion? They were quite . . . different.

The grandfatherly older man seemed benign, and Early thought he was probably harmless, although he was thrilled, intrigued, and mystified by his voice. He didn't think the younger man was dangerous but recognized that he was not someone to be trusted or tested.

The most recent addition, the shifty little guy with nervous eyes, was straight out of a bad gangster movie—a walking cliché. All in all, this was shaping up to be the most interesting Friday afternoon Early had ever experienced.

Chapter 33

Sometimes You Gotta Let Go

Vinnie Carlisle had grown accustomed to being in charge of whatever situation he found himself in; he liked being the Boss. But now, in this dinky little coffee shop with this peculiar assortment of people, he couldn't figure out what was going on or how he fit in. How did the elegant man know his name? And how in the world did he keep that linen suit wrinkle-free?

Facing the Adversary of God, he said, "Who the hell are you supposed to be?"

Satan gave him a smile an alligator would have envied but didn't say a word. The Old Man said, "Yes. That is precisely the question we are here to answer." Then, turning to Satan, He said, "Who are you supposed to be?"

In that moment, Narni returned to the table and put a piece of lemon icebox pie and a cup of coffee in front of Vinnie, who didn't acknowledge her, the pie, or the coffee. She waited for a few seconds and then with acid in her voice said, "You're welcome," and resumed her seat.

"Thank you, Narni. It does not fit into the image he wants to project to be grateful for anything."

"Whoa! You don't know anything about me, you old fool!" Vinnie exclaimed.

Narni resumed her seat and murmured a little more loudly than she meant to: "You might be surprised."

The Old Man turned His attention to His stylish associate. "Mr. Walter Johnson has offered his hand in friendship to you. What will you do?"

The Adversary shifted in his chair. "What, are You just going to ignore this . . . Vinnie Carlisle?"

"No, I will not ignore him, as I do not ignore any of my children. Nor do I wish to allow you to distract from this remarkable moment.

Mr. Elkins is here for a purpose as well, but his time has not yet come. Has a human ever, in all of your many sad, dark, lonely years as My Adversary, invited your friendship?"

"No—as You well know—no. Not if they knew who I am."

"Yet this extraordinary man has just done so. What will you do?"

Lucifer looked at Walter, and the rest of the table followed his eyes. Walter timidly held out his hand again with an apprehensive smile. There was a long pause until Mary Elizabeth said, "He don't want to be your friend, Dub. He don't want nothin' to do with you, with people like us."

Walter's smile faded somewhat and now seemed more forced. His eyes held Satan's, but he asked Mary Elizabeth, "Well, what *do* he want?"

"Yes, Walter, that is the right question: What does the Prince of Darkness want?"

The attention of the table focused on Satan. It seemed to Narni that he was smaller now, not so attractive—or so dangerous—as he had been earlier. She felt . . . sorry for him.

This idea brought her back to the pressing question—she still didn't know who these two men were. She wasn't ready to believe they were who they claimed to be, but she wasn't sure they were lying, either. How could the older man have known so much about her life, about her mother? But if the Old Man was God, then the younger man would have to be Satan, and how could she feel sorry for *him*? A memory of her sometime-boyfriend Jeremy broke through—just as ill-timed as the real Jeremy—a memory of him singing an old Rolling Stones song.

> Please allow me to introduce myself
> I'm a man of wealth and taste
> I've been around for a long, long year
> Stole many a man's soul to waste.

As the song went on, there were several historical references that Narni couldn't remember, and something about Jesus. But the words that had always caught her attention were toward the end:

So if you meet me, have some courtesy
Have some sympathy, and some taste
Use all your well-learned politesse
Or I'll lay your soul to waste.

The name of the song was "Sympathy for the Devil." Jeremy said it was a classic, but Narni thought he played it because the old people at the Hound Dog seemed to like it, the chords were easy, and—most importantly—it wasn't Elvis. The old patrons at their office parties could sing along with the chorus: "Pleased to meet you, hope you guessed my name."

This man's name was Ben Shachar, the Son of the Morning, Narni thought. He was Lucifer, Satan, the Adversary of God. And he had never had a friend. She put together all the courage she could find and hoped to find some more as she said, "Excuse me, sir—Ben—surely it couldn't hurt to have a friend?"

Ben looked at the Old Man, who nodded his encouragement. Then he looked at Narni for the first time and said, "It is not in my nature to . . . care for someone else."

"But can you change? Does that have to be your nature? What if you did care?"

Millie Ketchum cleared her throat, preparing to say something, but after she had everyone's attention, she changed her mind.

The Old Man broke the silence by looking at Ben Shachar and repeating Narni's question: "What if you did care, Ben? What would happen then?"

As Ben searched for a response, the Old Man turned to Millie Ketchum and asked, "What if *you* cared, Millie?" Millie was quietly scandalized that he would ask such a question, but then she had to consider it. It had been a long time since she had cared about anyone other than herself.

Then He turned to Vinnie Carlisle and said, "What if *you* cared, Danny?" He gestured around the circle gathered at the tables and looked each of them in their eyes. "What if you cared? What would happen then?"

It was a long, tense moment, and it was a surprise to most of them that it was Early Miller who answered, and with such honesty it brought tears to Narni's eyes. "Well, we might get hurt."

"Why?"

Everyone was looking at Early, expecting him to say more; he hadn't even meant to say anything. "Well, I guess if you're gonna care, you're gonna have to let your walls down, y'know?"

"Yes. I know."

Ben said, "It is costly to love."

"It is costly to love, yes, and risky. But what is the point of life without Love? Surely it is worth the cost, worth the risk, to love, to be loved freely and openly. Surely it is why I Am, why any of you live."

"You make it sound so simple," Narni objected.

"No, Sweet Heart. It is never simple. Nothing about love is ever simple or easy. It is, however, always worth the effort, always worth the risk."

Mary Elizabeth, who knew about the risk of love, was crying; Walter put his arm over her shoulder and drew her into his embrace. He said, "Teach us how to love, Lord."

"No, child, you do not need Me to teach you how to love. You just need to do it, all of you. Just love. Just forget about yourself and put someone else's needs and welfare before your own. You do not need to know more; you just need to do what you know how to do. Love as you have been loved. Love all of my children because they are my children. And forgive. Forgive others, forgive yourself."

"It's not that easy!" Narni insisted.

"No. I Am not saying that it is easy or simple. I Am saying that it is worth the effort and worth the risk."

Narni said, "Hmm."

God continued, "Before that terrible night, before your father killed your mother, your life was sweeter, less complicated."

"Yeah, so?"

"You played tag with the children in your neighborhood. Do you remember?"

"I hated tag!"

"Yes, because the other children were older than you, faster than you. Everybody but Fran."

"She was youngest and littlest."

"And you did not want to leave her behind."

Remembering, Narni whispered, "No."

"But playing tag was fun. All the children loved it."

"It wasn't fun for me and Fran."

"You hated tag because you never left base."

"They would have caught us if we had! And I could never catch them! I'd be stuck being It."

"You have to leave base sometimes, or it is not much of a game. You are safe if you stay on base, but you are never really playing."

"Like You played tag when You were a kid?"

"I was there the whole time. I stood with you on base. I ran with the others, chasing, being chased."

"I didn't see You there."

"Yet I was there. Your awareness does not affect reality, only your perception of reality. I was always there, in all the laughter and in all the tears."

"Okay, I got it. So?" She hadn't meant to be rude, but the Old Man didn't seem to mind.

"You put too much importance on being safe, on being sure. You need to let go of what is safe if you really want to play the game. Life is not just about surviving it."

Walter said, "Ain't none of us gonna survive."

"Life is an adventure. There are times to play it safe, and other times you have to take a chance. Sometimes you have to let down your guard; sometimes you have to trust."

Mary Elizabeth said, "He's sayin' sometimes you gotta let go what's safe and run around a little bit."

The Soul of Kindness gently added, "You may want to give that young man another chance."

Narni was stunned. "What do you know about that?"

The Old Man smiled His daybreak smile. "You are continually surprised to find out what I know."

"He hurt me."

"He hurt your pride. And now that pride is in your way and will not allow you to talk to the man you love."

Narni wanted to protest, and she would have if she had not known that what He said was true.

They sat in silence for a long moment, each of them taking this in, each of them in their own way. Millie Ketchum was determined that she was not going to cry, but her tear ducts betrayed her and her nose began to run. Mac offered her a bandanna, which she looked at suspiciously, so he whispered, "It's clean." She took the bandanna and grudgingly nodded her thanks.

Then God said to all of them, "Our friend Narni asked Ben a wonderful question: 'What if you cared?' What would happen then? What if you loved? What if you believed what you claim to believe? What if you decided to forgive those who have hurt you? What if you decided to forgive yourself? What would happen then?"

The little bell at the door rang, announcing the arrival of five more people into Fuddy's World Famous Pie Emporium; Narni recognized all but one. She was surprised at how glad she was to see her boyfriend Jeremy Adams. She wondered whether she would be able to forgive him and to love him. And, she admitted to herself, there were things he would have to forgive her for as well. She couldn't wait to tell him what had been going on at Fuddy's that afternoon.

The next person she saw was Jeremy's worthless friend Tucker, missing a shoe, bleeding from a severe-looking scratch on his ankle, still wearing a red Santa hat and bedraggled white beard, and being held with one arm behind his back by Mr. Doyle, the old bank guard. Mr. Doyle had always been friendly to Narni, and she wondered what sort of trouble Tucker had gotten himself into this time. More to forgive, thought Narni.

The woman who came in with them didn't seem to have anything to do with them. Maybe she just wanted a slice of pie, and now she was getting all caught up in . . . whatever this was. Narni recognized her. She couldn't remember her name, but she thought she was a nice person. Her only interaction with her had been uncomfortable, though—she worked with Dr. Whitaker, her dentist; she'd cleaned

Narni's teeth a few months before, and while it wasn't pleasant, the hygienist had tried to make it as painless as possible.

Behind them came one last person. He was tall and thin and had long, graying hair. He wore a tailored suit and expensive-looking shoes. The moment their eyes met, Narni knew that her father had found her. He did not recognize her, but despite her best efforts, she remembered him.

Chapter 34

An Accidental Gathering
of Innocence and Guilt

Jeremy Adams wished he could be somewhere else. Actually, he wished he could be someone else. He wished he could go back twenty-four hours and do things differently. He wished he could have half an hour alone with Narni, to either apologize enough so she would take him back or let her break it off with him forever. He wished he'd never met Grayson Tucker or gotten involved with his dumb Santa scheme. He wished all the people at Fuddy's would stop looking at him. The crazy bank guard pushed him into the coffee shop and growled, "All right, which one of you is Nonny, or Nanny?"

Narni stood up and raised her hand. "Hi, Mr. Doyle. It's Narni—Narni Pivens. I see you at the bank every Monday morning."

The change in Mickey Doyle was immediate and total, from the gruff, tough cop on the beat to a little boy with a crush on the prettiest girl on the playground. "Oh," he said, obviously flustered. "Hey."

Jeremy felt a rush of jealousy and reminded himself that he had squandered that right. He knew he ought to do something or say something or . . . something. But all he could do was stand there, looking and feeling totally lost.

A few minutes ago, everything had been more or less under control. He'd been in the comics shop, alone all day, so bored that he'd managed to stuff twenty-six peanut M&M's into his mouth—and then it had all fallen apart. First the crazy old bank guard had busted in and forced him to lie down on the floor with a mouthful of half-chewed peanuts. Then his sometime friend Tucker had slipped in, trying to avoid the police, and the bank guard had shifted his focus—and his pistol—onto him. The bank guard had ordered both of them to lie down and then called the police using Jeremy's cell phone.

Tucker had whispered frantically, "What are we going to do, man?" and Jeremy had said, "We're going to jail, Tucker. We're going to jail for a long time."

But the guard hung up in disgust after getting the answering machine and told them to get on their feet. "All right, let's go. If the police are too busy to answer their damn phone, I'll just take you to them."

He'd motioned with his pistol that Jeremy and Tucker should go through the front door, apparently not realizing that the bank was just across the back alley from the comics shop. When they left the shop, Jeremy had turned to the right, and Tucker had stomped down on the guard's shoe and run off to the left. Jeremy was stunned as he stood there watching his friend evade the law, and then the guard grabbed him, twisted his arm behind his back, and pushed the revolver into his throat.

He'd called out, "Hey, punk—you forgot something!"

Tucker stopped before he got to the corner. "You gonna shoot him? I don't think so."

The guard twisted Jeremy's arm harder until Jeremy let out a little moan. He yelled back, "No, I'm not gonna shoot him. I'm the good guy, right? But I'm not so good that I'm not gonna hurt this guy." He twisted Jeremy's arm even harder; Jeremy cried out again and wondered why his arm or elbow hadn't already broken. "So what're you gonna do, punk? You gonna run off and let your friend take the heat for you?" Jeremy was genuinely surprised to see Tucker raise his hands in surrender and start to walk back toward them.

The guard had yelled, "Down on the ground!" Jeremy started to lie down again, but the guard hissed, "Not you, idiot." After Tucker was on the ground, the guard said to Jeremy, "Call the police again."

Jeremy checked his pockets before remembering that the guard had put his phone on the shop counter by the cash register. "You left my phone in there. I can go get it if you want."

"You think I'm stupid? You think I'd just let you go in there and hope you'd come back?"

"No, sir."

"We'll just collect your little friend and walk to the bank. I can't wait to see Lieutenant Snotnose's face when I bring you clowns in."

Jeremy and the guard had gotten Tucker back on his feet when another man came crossing Jefferson Street. He looked to be in his late fifties, maybe early sixties; he was handsome in a rough, suspicious sort of way: longish, graying, somewhat greasy hair, well dressed, and stylishly a week or so past a shave. Jeremy didn't know him, but at the same time he thought he looked familiar. There was something about his eyes . . .

The guard held his gun behind Tucker's back and now twisted Tucker's arm. He'd stopped to let the man go into the coffee shop, but the man had come up to them and said, "Hello, officer. This man owes me money."

Tucker had groaned at that point and murmured, "Just when you think the day couldn't get any worse." Then, more audibly, he said, "Look, Mr. P.—I can explain. I'm trying to get you the money, I swear."

"This kid tried to rob the bank," said the guard. "I'm taking him in."

The new guy had looked a little alarmed, apparently noticing the gun for the first time. "You the police?"

"Nah. Used to be, retired now. Move along, sir."

"I just need a few minutes with your little friend, here."

"You can visit him in jail."

"No, thank you. That would not be . . . convenient for me. He owes me ten thousand dollars."

At that point, Jeremy had said, "I thought it was eight!" and the familiar-looking stranger had said, "Well, interest, collection expenses . . . it adds up."

In that moment, Jeremy had recognized the seed of an idea and known he couldn't wait until it came into full bloom. "Collection expenses, like hiring some mobsters from Memphis to come down and get your money?" He glanced at the bank guard to see if the seed had sprouted at all and was gratified to see that it had.

"Mobsters?" the bank guard growled. He looked at the stranger and said, "What's he talking about?"

The man looked surprisingly innocent as he said, "I have no idea. I just stopped for . . ."—he looked at the sign over the door—"a slice of pie."

Tucker entered the conversation then, saying, "It's true, officer. I lost six thousand dollars to this man in a card game in Memphis. I couldn't pay, so I ran. He sent Vinnie Carlisle to collect for him. That's why I was trying to rob your bank, sir—so I could pay Mr. P. here, so they wouldn't kill me or break my legs or something."

Jeremy was impressed with Tucker's persuasiveness, and apparently the bank guard was, too. He was certainly tempted by the possibility of making a bigger bust. The guard said, "All right. You're coming with me." He motioned all three of them, an accidental gathering of innocence and guilt, toward the corner with his pistol and said, "Let's go."

But the man didn't move. "No, I don't believe so. You have no authority here. You're not the police, and I have done nothing wrong. I am the one who has been wronged—this man owes me money."

At that moment, Jeremy had said to the guard, "Hey, look—we can go into Fuddy's and call the police from there. My . . . friend Narni works there—you can use her phone." The bank guard made a fateful decision and said, "All right. We can all go in the pie shop and wait for the police there." He'd turned to the stranger and said, "If you ain't done nothin' wrong, you got nothin' to worry about. Let's go."

They'd all stood there for a moment until the guard said to Jeremy, "You first, then Santa, then this guy," nodding to Mr. P. Jeremy had just pulled the door open when a woman walked up, and everybody instinctively stepped back to let her through. She'd smiled at Jeremy and said, "Age before beauty." Jeremy had hesitated, not knowing what to do, until the guard shoved him through the door before asking for Nonny or Nanny.

Now Narni was in front of them, as lovely as a sunrise on the beach, the most beautiful sight Jeremy had ever seen. She'd glanced at him before saying, "Hi, Mr. Doyle," and his heart had swelled;

maybe the damage could be repaired. But when she'd gone on to say, "It's Narni—Narni Pivens," Jeremy felt the stranger beside him tensing and heard him take a sharp breath.

Chapter 35

Don't Forget the Pitchfork

The Lord God Almighty, Creator of heaven and earth, stood and spread His arms in welcome. "Ah, very good. We are all here." Then He said to the five newcomers, "Please come and join us." He looked at His eternal adversary and said, "Ben, will you help our friend Narni bring some coffee and pie, please?" Before Satan could protest or answer, He said to Narni, "We will need four cups of coffee and five slices of lemon icebox pie, please. Young Jeremy would rather have milk, I Am sure." Then he turned to Walter and said, "Would you and Thomas bring up another table and five more chairs, please?"

Narni, Walter, and Mac all stood to do what they'd been asked to do; Satan sat for a moment and then followed Narni into the kitchen. Narni tried not to look at the man she thought was her father, but she couldn't help a quick peek. He was looking at her intensely. She thought, "The Old Man said my father was coming and that I ought to forgive him! But how could I possibly forgive him? I don't care if He's God or not, that's too much to ask."

Trudie Svoboda came over to stand beside Early Miller, who stood when she walked up. She put her hand on his arm and whispered, "What's going on?"

He whispered back, "Hell if I know." Then he pulled out his chair and said, "Come sit here with me. I'll try to catch you up as much as I can."

Mickey Doyle would not have said that he was a religious man. He would have said that he had seen and done too much to believe in a just and merciful God. He would have said that he believed in the power of the law, upheld by force when necessary. He would have said that he'd prayed when his sweet Elizabeth was lying in that damn hospital bed for months, but he didn't really know who he thought he was talking to, and she had died anyway. He would have said that the world was full of religious nuts, people who claimed to know

God's will, hear God's voice, or see God; he would have said that they were selling something he wasn't buying or that they were either full of it, lying, or easily manipulated.

But when he saw the Man in the gray sweater and heard His extraordinarily compelling voice, he knew he was going to have to rethink a lot of what he would have said before that moment. He shifted from one foot to the other, bashful to approach this oddly powerful man, until the Old Man nodded and extended His left hand in welcome, directing the bank guard to the chair where the one He'd called Ben had been sitting.

Mickey hesitated and wondered what was going on. He hadn't been bashful since he'd met Elizabeth, almost fifty years ago; there hadn't been any room for bashful in Vietnam or on the Memphis police department. Then the Man spoke directly to him—"Come and join us"—and Mickey Doyle felt like a child again as he took the chair.

It occurred to Tucker that he could run for it, with the bank guard acting all goofy all of a sudden and sitting by the old guy. He slid toward the door, but Mr. P. caught his arm and whispered, "I'm not done with you yet, boy." Just then the old man said, "Let him go, Luke. If he doesn't want to stay, he is free to leave." Mr. P. released his arm, and Tucker knew he could leave, but now something compelled him to stay. Maybe it was just curiosity, maybe it was the loss of blood, maybe he didn't think he would get very far and he'd rather be at Fuddy's than in a jail cell.

The Old Man said, "Luke, Grayson, Jeremy, come and sit with us. We are all friends here, and we have a mystery to solve. The coffee and the pie are on Me." Mr. P.—Luke—went and sat down in one of the chairs that the priest had pulled to the tables. Tucker followed, picking a chair as far away from the two mobsters as possible, which unfortunately put him right next to the bank guard, who didn't seem to mind. Or notice.

Jeremy sat next to Tucker to show a little support, and also seeking some. Only two chairs remained—the one on his left and the other between Mr. P. and a guy who looked like a caricature of a gangster from a movie Jeremy would not have watched. Jeremy hoped Narni would come and sit next to him; something weird was going on at Fuddy's this afternoon. He wondered what was taking her so long with that shifty-looking Ben.

"Four cups of coffee, five pieces of lemon pie, and a glass of milk," murmured Narni, thinking out loud. Then she turned to Ben and said, "I don't really need any help, but thank you."

"I don't mind," said Satan. "I'm glad to assist."

She was pouring the milk when she remembered how odd it was that the Old Man knew Jeremy would rather have milk. She turned to Ben and asked, "How does he know that?"

"How does who know what? Try a few nouns."

"How does . . . the Old Man know that Jeremy would want to drink milk with his pie? What if Jeremy decided he wanted tea instead? Sometimes he drinks tea."

"He knows."

"But how? How can he know all that stuff, about my mother and . . . my father, and Dub's name, and about Miss Mully's daughter, and that Jeremy doesn't drink coffee?" She hesitated, then plunged into what she was afraid would be a deep pool with no lifeguards, "Who is he, really? And who are you?"

"Well," said Ben, seeming less comfortable, less sensual, and somehow more likeable, "it's complicated. Why are you asking me?"

"Because you know, don't you?"

"We don't normally reveal ourselves to humans; He says it interferes with your freedom to choose. But He Himself has acknowledged who He is today, or at least hinted at it, so . . ."

Narni was stunned again. She repeated his words: "'Don't normally reveal ourselves to *humans*?' Oh my . . . God!" She shook her head, trying and failing to clear her mind. "He is God, like . . . God? And you're the Devil, like the real Devil?" Ben Shachar said nothing, just smiled his reptilian smile; Narni stepped back, her hands protecting her chest. "But you don't look like the Devil!"

"And how should I look to meet your expectations?"

"Well, you know—red, with horns . . ." She trailed off, hearing how ridiculous she sounded.

"And a pointed tail and a pitchfork. Don't forget the pitchfork."

"Well, yeah—all that."

"Where did you get those ideas?"

Narni shrugged.

"Throughout history, humans have been unwilling to accept that they do not know, so they have simply made things up. They assumed it would be better to say something absurd than to admit that they don't have an idea of what is true. It doesn't say anywhere in your precious Bible that I should be red or have horns or a tail. Red for the pits of fiery flames, I suppose, horns and cloven feet from the Greek god Pan, and a pitchfork from . . . well, who knows? Poseidon's trident, perhaps? It's all ridiculous."

Narni's mind did not seem to be working properly. "But . . . this is not possible!"

"Is it so unbelievable that God and Satan actually exist? Did you think that just because it was something people have believed in for centuries, it must automatically be imaginary? Ridiculous and arrogant."

Narni felt scolded. She was being asked to accept so many things: God and Satan were having lemon icebox pie in the coffee shop she worked in. Her father, who had murdered her mother, was now in that same shop with her goofy but loveable boyfriend, who had tried to step on her dream of going to New York, and his goofy and unlovable dopehead friend Tucker Claus. There was Mr. Doyle from the bank and some greasy gangster guy from Memphis. Miss Mully had a daughter with cerebral palsy, and Dub had served in Korea, and a preacher had just wandered in out of nowhere with his cute lawyer friend, and that old battleship Mrs. Ralph are-you-flipping-*kidding*-me Ketchum was finally quiet for once. And now *Narni* was being scolded for the theological assumptions of centuries of religious scholars who hadn't been able to admit that they didn't know?

Ben was about to say something else, but Narni showed him the palm of her hand and said, "Shut up. Just shut the hell up. It's not my fault I didn't recognize you—you haven't made it easy for us, y'know."

Again, the alligator smile. "It is not my job to make it easy for you—quite the opposite, in fact."

Narni put the coffees and slices of pie on the tray with Jeremy's glass of milk, adding a small pitcher of cream and packets of sugar and sweeteners in a little bowl. Ben Shachar, the Adversary of God, stood in front of the door, blocking her way.

"But if you will listen, I will say this. You are a remarkable young woman, and if Jeremy is too pig-headed to come crawling back to you, he is an utter fool. Trust your heart, Sarah. Trust your heart."

By the time she'd doled out the coffee and pie, there was only one chair left, right next to Jeremy. She wanted to rail at the unfairness of it, but she had to admit that she was glad.

She sat, and he leaned over to whisper something—an apology, probably, but she said, "It's okay," and kissed him on the cheek. She looked over at Ben, who winked at her. Jeremy buried his face in her neck and sobbed.

Chapter 36

Hope You Guessed My Name

The Old Man in the gray sweater looked around the cluster of tables where they were sitting. To His left was Mickey Doyle the bank guard, then Grayson Tucker the bank robber, then Jeremy Adams and the precious Narni Pivens. Continuing the circle clockwise were Millie Ketchum, Danny Royce Elkins (known to some as Vinnie Carlisle), Ben Shachar (who had many names), Luke Pivens, Mac McBride, Trudie Svoboda, Early Miller, Walter Johnson, and sweet Mary Elizabeth Sims.

He loved them all.

The Lord God held up His coffee cup and said, "Friends, a toast!" Everyone held up their coffee cups, except Jeremy, who held up a glass of milk, either half full or half empty, and Vinnie Carlisle, who was not generally given to doing what was expected of him. "To life, and to love."

Each of them made some response or another.

Mickey Doyle held up his cup and said, "To life, and to love!" feeling strangely more hopeful than he had since before he enlisted. In that magical moment, he missed Elizabeth, but he felt somehow assured that she was all right.

Tucker looked around to see what Vinnie Carlisle and Mr. P. were doing. He held up his cup because everybody except Mr. P. was doing it, but he didn't say anything because Mr. C. didn't.

Jeremy held up his glass and felt Narni's hand take his other hand. He would have said something, but he was choking down tears of relief and gratitude. He squeezed her hand and wished he would never have to let it go.

Narni winced a little at the pressure from Jeremy's hand, but she knew he meant it to be a loving gesture, and she loved him for it. She said, "To life, and to love!" and meant it fully. She felt her father's eyes on her and determined to ignore him.

Mrs. Ralph Ketchum, now exposed as Millie, held up her cup of coffee and mumbled the words, because that's what you do when someone makes a toast, and still wondered what in the world was going on.

Vinnie Carlisle sneered at the Old Man and muttered, "What the hell is this?" He left his cup untouched and broadened his sneer to include everybody in the circle. He saw that nobody was paying him any attention and wondered how he could sneer more conspicuously.

Ben Shachar lifted his cup of coffee and said, *"To life!"* loudly enough for everyone to hear what he said and what he had not said. He was sitting at a table with these animals that God had imbued with spirit and free will, and . . . and he had to admit it was not so bad as he would have thought.

Luke Pivens's eyes had rarely strayed from Narni since he'd heard her say her name. He had come because he didn't trust Carlisle, but now, by a most peculiar coincidence, he found himself in the presence of his daughter, and he was trying to sort out what that would mean for himself and for her. He lifted his coffee cup because she had and whispered, "Love."

The Rev. Mac McBride had been feeling goosebumps constantly for at least the last fifteen minutes. He believed in God, he believed in Jesus, and he believed in spirituality. He knew that people had religious experiences, but to this point he been more comfortable with other people having them and writing about them so he could read their words. He knew he was now having his very own mystical experience, and he was enjoying it. He decided he would go with it even though he couldn't understand it: "To life, and to love!"

Trudie Svoboda had no clue and didn't know where she might find one. The dental office was closed while the dentist was away visiting family, and Trudie had been at a loss all day. She'd been glad to see Father Mac in the coffee shop and was grateful that Early had invited her to sit with him, but she had no idea who most of these other people were. Still, she recognized a standard social cue and lifted her cup of coffee and said, "To life, and to love!"

Early Miller knew he was not going to figure this out any time soon. It would take some serious thought, maybe a conversation with

Mac, maybe over something strong. Maybe a couple of conversations with something very strong. But for now, he was sitting with Trudie, and they weren't talking about flossing or softball, and that was just fine with him. "To life, and to love!"

Walter Johnson had been lost even to himself for decades. Now he was himself again, which he knew was nothing short of a miracle. He wished everybody would just be quiet so they could all hear God talk some more. He held up his cup and said, "To life, and to love!" just like most everybody else.

Mary Elizabeth Sims was completely overwhelmed—by the remarkable change in her friend Dub, by the talk about her daughter, by her conversation with the Devil, and by God. It was all too much. For years she had forgotten that she was Mary Elizabeth Sims and had tried to forget that she had a daughter once. It was so long ago, and such a hard time, a painful time. She didn't ever want to forget her sweet Tallulah, but she didn't want to remember that pain, that horrible, helpless pain. But now she was sitting with God—God His own self—and it was all going to be all right. She was crying, but she felt like laughing; she held up her cup, too, filled with emotion to say anything.

When all the cups were back on the tables, God smiled and said, "Thank you, children. I Am glad you are all here."

Vinnie Carlisle stood abruptly and yelled at Him. "Who the hell do you think you are, old man? Are you some kind of cheap magician or something? What are you trying to pull here?"

The Old Man's smile was undiminished, but before Vinnie could speak again, Ben stood and took him by the collar of his shirt, lifting him slightly off the floor. "Be silent, fool. You are in the presence of beings that your meager mind cannot fathom. You will show respect."

"Ben, thank you, but I do not need to be protected. We cannot force Mr. Elkins to respect, do you not see?"

"I do not see why You tolerate such . . . insolence. I may not be able to force him to respect You, but I can force him to behave respectfully."

"I Am sure you could, but it does no good and could well do harm. I do not want anyone to pretend to respect or to have faith or to love because they are afraid of Me or of you."

"You realize, of course, that the churches are selling faith through fear every Sunday."

"Yes, I Am aware that some of the churches use such tactics. As I say, it does no good and could well do harm. Now I would like for you to put Mr. Elkins down. He is not breathing well in his present predicament."

Satan let go of Vinnie Carlisle's collar, and he sat down heavily, gasping for breath.

"Now," said the Lord God, "We have come to a unique moment, and I Am glad that you are all here. I want to introduce you to my son, Ben Shachar. Perhaps some of you know him already." Vinnie Carlisle sniffed with a sour look. "Now, Ben, my question still stands. Walter's offer is still there. It is time for you to decide."

"Decide?"

"Will you at last come Home? Will you reconcile yourself to the nature of creation and walk again in the love of your Father?"

Tucker leaned across Jeremy to whisper to Narni, "Ben left his home and father?" Narni whispered back, "Yeah, a long time ago. But . . . I guess his father still loves him and is willing to forgive him. A lot."

Tucker said, "Wow. That's like a story in the Bible, right?"

Mary Elizabeth spoke up now. "Lord, no! You can't just take him back! How can you trust him after all he's done?"

"He is my son," God said simply. "Thank you, child, for wanting to protect Me, but it is not necessary. It is ever my choice to trust, to believe, to hope. I choose, even now, to love. It is Who I Am."

Mary Elizabeth was indignant. "But you said he was your adversary. You and him been at war since the Garden of Eden! You threw him out of heaven with lightning or some such—you know he's just gonna cheat and steal and lie if you let him back! You takin' a big chance!"

"It is risky to love, yes, and can be costly. But as I heard a wise woman quite recently say, 'Sometimes you have to let go of what is safe and run around a little bit.'"

Mary Elizabeth leaned over to Walter and whispered, "Well, somethin' like that, anyway."

Mickey Doyle raised his hand, like a little boy in the second grade. God called on him, "Yes, Michael?"

"Sir, I am . . . afraid, I guess, because I don't know what's happening. And I'm afraid I'm not really supposed to be here. If you want me here, I'll be glad to stay, but could you tell us what's going on?

God laughed, and the sound of it filled Fuddy's World Famous Pie Emporium from wall to wall, from floor to ceiling. Only Vinnie and Luke were not lightened by the laugh; even Satan smiled, if only a little.

"Yes, of course. You need not be afraid. I will tell you the Truth and leave it to you to choose whether or not you are willing to believe it. I Am known by many names, but no matter what I Am called, I Am the Creator."

Millie Ketchum was struggling, but she really did want to know: "Creator of what?"

Her priest recited the first article of the Nicene Creed, which he had said for most of his life but never meant as fully as he did now: "We believe in one God, the Father, the Almighty, maker of heaven and earth, of all that is, seen and unseen."

Millie said, "Oh." And then on second thought, she asked Mac, "Is that possible?"

Mac answered, "Did you think God was hypothetical?"

God resumed His answer to Mickey Doyle. "And this is my son Ben. In the writing of the Hebrew prophet Isaiah, he is referred to as 'Helel ben Shachar' which is translated 'Shining One' or 'the Son of the Morning.' He has also been called Lucifer, Satan, Mephistopheles, and the Devil, among many other names."

People reacted around the tables, nearly simultaneously.

Mary Elizabeth shook her head sadly and said, "Don't trust him, Lord."

Walter looked at Satan and offered him a nervous smile.

Early Miller said, "WHAT?"

Trudie took Early's arm to pull him back into his chair, whispering, "Hold on now, there's gotta be some explanation. Just wait a minute."

Mac crossed himself and then wondered why; he had never been High Church as a rule.

Luke Pivens steepled his fingers under his nose. This was getting interesting, and he wondered how he would be able to work it to his advantage.

Ben Shachar nodded solemnly, acknowledging his father's introduction.

Vinnie stood, yelling, "You're crazy as hell, all of you! I'm out of here!" But he did not leave, and when no one moved to restrain him or made any indication that they'd heard him, he sat back down.

Millie Ketchum was having trouble catching her breath. Everything seemed upside down. She looked around for someone else to ask, someone to talk to, and realized there was no one here or anywhere else. She was alone, as she'd always thought she'd wanted to be. Until now.

Narni leaned over to Jeremy and quoted Mick Jagger: "Pleased to meet you, hope you guessed my name."

Jeremy looked at her in disbelief and whispered back, "The devil? Like . . . the actual devil?" Narni nodded.

Grayson Tucker decided that he would like to wake up now, that he wasn't enjoying this dream. He pinched his arm and said, "Ow!"

Mickey Doyle waited for the commotion to subside and said, "Thank you, Lord. But why are we here?"

When God spoke again, everyone was still and quiet. "It may be that I will need one of you to help Me." There was another buzz around the tables, and when it calmed, He continued, "Ben? What will you do? Will you come Home?"

Everyone looked at Ben, who looked only at God. *"No, sir. I . . . I can't."*

"You can, Ben. It may be that will not. Your pride is in your way."

Jeremy didn't understand why Narni squeezed his hand just then, but he didn't mind in the least.

"But these . . . humans reject You, Sir. They have forgotten You."

"Not all, not all. They do not see spiritual reality as clearly as the angels do. For you, I Am unmistakable. They cannot be so sure."

"I wish it were otherwise, Lord, but . . . no. I will not."

Narni felt the tears on her face before she knew she was crying. "But Ben . . ." She stopped as she realized that everyone was looking at her. The Old Man nodded His encouragement, and she continued, "You know your Father loves you. Why would you want to reject that love because we may or may not see that He is . . . that He is God the Creator?"

"It is His decision to give you His spirit that I must reject! You are not worthy of His love!"

"Worthy?" she responded with a fury that surprised her. "No, I am not worthy! Neither are you, Ben Shachar! No one has ever been *worthy* of the love of God, you idiot!" The other people around the tables were astonished, motionless, speechless. Narni looked around at all of them. "Well, have we? Other than Jesus, who I guess was God anyway—I mean, have any of us ever deserved for God to love us?"

Mary Elizabeth said, "No, you're right, Sweet Pea. Ain't none of us never done nothin' to deserve that kind of love. He ain't lovin' us 'cause we worthy—He's lovin' us 'cause He chooses to. It's just . . . I guess it's just Who He is."

Chapter 37

Let It Be as You Say

They sat for a long moment, God and Satan and the twelve witnesses. Then Walter stood. Mary Elizabeth whispered, "Where you goin'?"

Walter said, "He ain't never answered *my* question." He walked around the tables and stopped when he came to Ben, holding out his hand. "I was still just . . . wonderin' if you was willin' to be my friend."

Ben looked at God, whose eyes twinkled as He laughed richly. Then he looked at Walter's outstretched hand as if he was considering taking it.

Danny Royce Elkins had become Vinnie Carlisle by embracing pride, hatred, resentment, and fear, all of which were on display as he said, "Oh, look—the widdle boy wants a widdle friend."

Walter took half a step back, his hand lowering a little, accepting the attitude he'd known his whole life. Ben stood and squared his shoulders to face Vinnie. "You owe that man an apology."

"Or what? You gonna beat it out of me?"

Ben Shachar seemed to stand a little taller, certainly more menacing. "I'd love to; thank you for suggesting it."

"Ben, think," said the Lord God. "It will do no good and may well do harm."

"So You're just going to let him be a jerk? Allow him to insult this good man?"

Vinnie sniggered. "This good man whose hand you won't even take? You hate 'em just as much as I do."

At this Mary Elizabeth came up out of her chair like a wave crashing ashore, an untamed force of nature. "Oh, *hell* no! I'm sorry Lord, but I ain't havin' *that!*" She stormed around the tables, building momentum as she went. She paused to remove one of her flip-flops and came brandishing it like a weapon. "I ain't havin' *none* of that!"

Vinnie realized that he was unarmed and that his men were not around to protect him from the crazy woman coming toward him. The sneer left his face in an instant, replaced by a look of panic. He looked at the delusional old man who'd been running things and said, "You gonna stop her?"

"She is free to make her choices, even as you are free to make yours. You chose to insult her friend, and I did not stop you; now it appears she is coming to strike you, and I will not stop her."

Ben grabbed Vinnie's left wrist to hold him for Mary Elizabeth, then turned to face his Father. "This may well do him some harm."

"Yes, but it may well do him some good."

Mary Elizabeth was holding the flip-flop in her left hand; she held it up as if to bring it down on Vinnie's head. He lifted his right arm to protect himself, and she stepped into a right undercut to his stomach that knocked the wind out of him. She waited for him to look up at her, and when he did, she hissed, "Now sit down and shut up, fool. Or I will be back."

Vinnie sat down.

Walter was trying not to laugh, but he wasn't trying too hard. He hugged Mary Elizabeth and thanked her. She said, "You ain't never gotta back down ever again, y'hear?" He nodded, and then he said to Ben, "Looks like you my friend whether you take my hand or not. Thank you."

"I'm not your . . . but you are welcome . . . my friend." And the Adversary of God extended his hand to Walter Lee Johnson, Private First Class, and repeated what Walter had said to him earlier: "I am . . . pleased to make your acquaintance, sir."

When Walter took his hand, Ben grimaced and breathed in sharply through his teeth, almost as if he expected some sort of existential collision of realities. When it didn't come, he looked at God like a child who'd just learned to ride his bike without training wheels.

"Well done, Ben. I Am glad for both of you. It is good to have a friend." Walter and Mary Elizabeth went back to their chairs, and God continued, "Now, Ben, you have come a small but significant step. Perhaps you now begin to see that there is something of value in these children of Mine."

"Perhaps."

"Walter did not have to befriend you, and he gained nothing by doing so. He chose to offer you friendship, knowing full well who you are, from the goodness of his heart."

"Goodness you put there."

"Yes, I put goodness in his heart, in all their hearts. Walter chose to use it. Others may choose to ignore it."

Ben said nothing, and God continued. "Having come this first hard step, perhaps you will consider taking the next one, which will be even more difficult. Can you accept My love? Can you at last come Home?"

Satan sat quietly, thinking; he was tempted. Then he said, "If I do, if I come Home, who would be your Adversary?"

"I would find someone who is willing to step into that role, to ensure that My children will be free to decide between love and fear, to either serve Me or serve themselves, because they choose it."

"Is that why these people are here? One of them would assume the duties of Satan?"

"Perhaps, if any wish it. There are one or two among them who would do quite well, would you not say?"

"And two or three who would be a disaster!"

"Yes, perhaps so."

"If I do this, if I . . . surrender myself to you, you would make one of these—"

"No. Let us be careful here. As I Am eternal, Love is eternal. Love has ever been, and will ever be, without beginning and without end. Love is stronger than hatred or fear. You are not surrendering; you are simply accepting My Love.

"I will not make any of these become Satan. I do not force; I do not make any of them do anything. I did not force Noah or Abraham or Jacob. I did not force you, Ben."

"But I have always been—"

"No, not always."

"But since I was cast out of heaven . . ."

"You have not always been My Adversary."

"But I've always . . . I don't understand, Lord."

"No. Now a time has come that you do understand. If you relinquish your role as Satan, you will resume the life you left behind to become My Adversary. You will die a human death and come Home."

Jeremy breathed, "Good Lord!"

Ben asked, "Resume the life I left behind?"

"Yes. The Satan before you found she could not continue after seeing the destruction of Hiroshima and Nagasaki. She tempted men in power to make terrible decisions that she could not bear, and she asked to come Home."

Narni asked, "She?"

Satan said, "But I am your eternal adversary!"

"Yes . . . and no. Satan is my eternal adversary, and you are Satan. But you have not always been Satan."

"How can that be? I don't understand!"

"It is difficult, I know."

Early Miller could have been a good lawyer if he'd been interested in it; he had the sort of mind that assimilates disparate facts into reasonable order. He said, "Let me see if I got this right." God motioned with His right hand that Early had the floor, and he continued. "This is God we're sitting with here, the real God, the Creator of the universe." God nodded serenely. "And over there is Satan, Ben something, the Adversary of God." Ben mirrored his Father's nod. "God needs an adversary in the same way that the judge needs a prosecutor and a defense attorney, not to escape justice but so that the judicial system is whole, complete." Again, Early looked at God, who nodded and spread His hands in agreement, encouraging him. "The problem is—well, I guess you could call it a problem if you need an Adversary—the problem is that God is Love, and God is eternal, so it stands to reason that Love is eternal, right?" There were several nods from the people around the tables. "Love is always offered, and eventually, love always wins. So . . ."

"Again, we need to be careful in our speech. You are doing quite well, but you are making an assertion I must put right. Some do not choose to be loved or to love; some choose themselves over all else."

Narni asked, "What happens to them?"

"They receive what they ask for; they live outside of My Love. You call it Hell."

She persisted, "So if we choose not to love You, You send us to Hell."

"No, Sweet Heart. If you choose to love yourself above all else, if you choose not to accept My Love, I honor that choice. But I Am forever offering My Love; the Harrowing of Hell is ever ongoing. As Christians teach it, I Am God the Father, I am the Holy Spirit, and I Am Jesus; I visit those who live in the Hell they make of their own guilt and despair. I do not send them there; I invite them to come out of it, to release their Hell so they can embrace Heaven."

"But what if they've been bad?" Trudie asked. "What if their sins are too great?"

"Is it too much to believe that I love all of My children all the time, no matter what, for all time?" He looked at Narni then and said, "There is no sin that cannot be forgiven by Love. Love, hope, and forgiveness are eternal."

Millie, lifelong Episcopalian and stalwart of the pews of St. Paul's, the parish's largest contributor, said, "Well, that hardly seems fair."

"Fair? Oh no, it is not meant to be fair. It is grace beyond measure, offered to all of My children equally."

Mac said, "It's like the story of the Prodigal Son—I mean, the older brother didn't think it was fair when his father threw the younger brother a feast. Or the story of the man who hired some workers in the early morning, others through the day, and finally some in the late afternoon, and paid them all the same." He realized that everyone was looking at him and concluded his homily. "Well, that wasn't fair, either."

Now Vinnie Carlisle stepped into the conversation. "So I can just do whatever the hell I want to do now and ask for forgiveness later and go to Heaven?"

"You are free, Danny Royce: free to do as you choose. Some of your choices may make it much more difficult for you to live in harmony with me, not because I will not forgive you, but the distance you put between yourself and Me will make it difficult for you to accept My forgiveness. In order for you to 'Go to Heaven,' you will need to turn yourself around, away from hate and fear and selfishness, to love and mercy and compassion. Hear me: you cannot bring bigotry and self-centered spite with you; you must set aside grievances and grudges to come Home. It is My will that must be done in Heaven, not yours."

Early wasn't through. "So the problem is when Satan accepts Your love, You need to find somebody else who is willing to be Satan."

"Precisely. Well said."

Early beamed.

Mac wondered, "How many Satans have there been?"

God answered, "One. But Satan has worn many human bodies, for a time."

Satan said, "I don't remember being human."

"No. That is part of the Arrangement." God looked around the tables. "If you choose to be Satan, you are fully the Adversary of God."

Mac said, "Until you choose not to be."

"Yes. With Satan, with all My children, I honor the choices you make."

Early whispered to Trudie, "It's like the Dread Pirate Roberts from The Princess Bride!"

Satan said, "I will . . . go back? Who was I before? Where will I be, and what year?"

"Part of the Arrangement is that you will not remember your previous life until you opt to return to it. Your choice in this moment is not between your life now and your life then but about whether you, having seen Me clearly and now knowing in full certainty the spiritual reality we share, wish to continue in your role as My Adversary or wish to live in Love."

"And I will die."

"Yes. You will die and come Home."

"Will they . . . will those who are Home know that I was Satan?"

"Yes, and they will love you for your service to Creation."

Love, hope, and forgiveness had come to life in Satan's heart, so long devoid of anything of the sort. He sat for a long moment, his head between his hands, clearly struggling, wrestling with himself, and made the decision. "I . . . I relinquish my role as the Adversary of God and pledge myself to serve and love You forever."

The Lord of Creation nodded. "Let it be as you say."

There was no thunder, no special effects, nothing extraordinary at all, but the world changed in a moment, and the fact that only those in Fuddy's World Famous Pie Emporium knew it made it no less consequential.

"Before you became My Adversary, you were Seaman Benjamin James Lanier, aviation mechanic aboard the USS *Bunker Hill*."

Ben took a sharp breath as the memories returned, "We called it the Holiday Express . . . we said she was the mightiest aircraft carrier in the US Navy."

"The *Bunker Hill* was part of the invasion of Okinawa in May 1945, when two kamikazes dropped their bombs and crashed into her. Three hundred and ninety-three of the crew were killed, and two hundred and sixty-four were wounded, including you, Ben. You were severely burned trying to extinguish the terrible fire. You reached out to Me from your hospital bed in Pearl Harbor, saying you would do anything I asked, if I could just get you back home to Lawson, Mississippi."

There were several gasps around the table now. "My husband had some cousins who were Laniers," said Millie Ketchum. "His grand-mother's brother was named Preston; they called him . . . ah, Lump, for some reason."

Ben wiped the tears from his eyes—when was the last time he'd cried? "Preston Lanier, Lump . . . was my daddy." Ben looked at God, and asked, "Is he—"

"Home."

"And Mama?"

"Home as well. And now, Ben," said God gently, "your time comes near. If you have anything to say to any of these, you should say it now."

"Thank you, Lord." Ben wiped his eyes with the back of his hand. "I want to say to all of you: live fully, without fear—each of you is a child of God. Live in joy, in love, and in wonder."

Narni Pivens went over to Ben Lanier and kissed him on his all-too-human cheek. "Thank you," she whispered. He held her tight for a moment and whispered back, "Forgive," and then he was simply no longer there.

Chapter 38

The Point of It All

Early Miller thought he must've missed something. "What? What happened to Ben?"

"Ben has come Home. Seaman First Grade Benjamin James Lanier died on May 23, 1945, in the Pearl Harbor Naval Hospital. He was posthumously awarded the Navy Cross and was buried with honors in Oakwood Memorial Cemetery north of town. His father Preston and his mother Margaret were buried beside him."

There was a moment of silence, some in respect and some in confusion. Then Jeremy asked, "So what happens now?"

"Now I want to determine if any of you are willing to take his place."

Mac was incredulous. "To be . . . Satan?"

"Yes. I need an Adversary."

"But why?" Narni wanted to know.

"I make choices as well, and even I must choose between what is good and what is not."

Millie asked, "What are the terms of the Arrangement?"

"Ah, very good. The terms are these: As Satan, you will be a purely a spiritual creature.

"You will not hunger or thirst; you will not age or die for as long as you choose to be My Adversary.

"You will no longer be who you have been or remember your previous life; you will be Satan, the eternal Adversary of God, who rebelled against Me.

"You will continue to be Satan until you relinquish the role, at which time your body will die, and you will be released to come Home, or to serve yourself elsewhere.

"Your duty as Satan will be to whisper, to persuade, to entice humanity toward darkness, away from My Light.

"You will not have the power to force anyone to do anything; I give you license only to tempt.

"As a spiritual being, you will exist beyond the boundaries of time and space; you will be able to influence multitudes individually and simultaneously.

"You will not enter into a human's mind; there never has been and never shall be an instance of 'demon possession'; that was only ever a clumsy attempt to explain what was not understood.

"You will not create evil; I alone Create. The role of Satan is to point to the hatred, fear, and selfishness within My children and make it seem more appealing than it is.

"You are not to become personally involved with any one individual or to reveal that you are Satan or a spiritual being.

"Now, My children, I will speak to each of you individually, and at the same time. No one other than Myself will hear the answers you give to the three questions I Am going to ask you, or hear the one question you may ask Me. Do you understand?"

Trudie said, "You're going to talk to us individually, all at the same time?"

"Yes. As I Am a spiritual being, I transcend time and space." Trudie shook her head in muddled incomprehension, and God added, "As physical creatures, you are limited to being in one place in any given moment. For Me as a spiritual being, all moments are now and all places are here."

Tucker exclaimed, "Wow!"

"Now I will give you a moment to consider the questions I Am going to ask you and to think carefully about the question you wish to ask Me. First, would you like to serve as the Adversary of God? Second, why do you think you would or would not be well suited to it? And finally, who besides yourself among the twelve of you would you think would be a good Satan? I will then answer the one question you would like to ask Me. Are there any questions about this process?"

"Yes . . . um, sir," stuttered Luke Pivens. "Do you mean I can ask You any question and you will answer it truthfully?"

"Yes. I Am the truth. But I will not tell you the date or the place of your death."

Luke feigned indignance. "That's not what I was going to ask!" God said nothing, and Luke continued, "But why wouldn't you tell me that, if I did ask it?"

"Because you should not know that. It is not love to tell you when or where you will die; such knowledge would distort the life you live. You live your life knowing that you will not live forever, but you should live each day as fully as you can. Knowing the date and the place of your death is more than you could manage."

"What, you think I'm too stupid to know the truth?"

Mary Elizabeth offered, "No—it'd be like explainin' a magnet to a mouse, that's all."

"Exactly. Your life is not a script in which you only read the lines written for you; you decide every day who you are and who you will be. You will die, as all humans must; whether that day comes tomorrow or far into the future is not as important as your willingness to forget yourself enough to love another."

There were no other questions, and God spoke to each of them.

God spoke to Mac McBride, who said, "Lord, I have given my whole life to serve You. If You call me to be Your Adversary, I will do the best I can.

"I don't know how well I would do being Satan, and I imagine there's a steep learning curve for any of us. I've always been a good student, so I guess that's what I would have to offer.

"This might sound weird, but I have the idea that Narni would be a good Satan—not because she's mean or bad but because she's not, and she's a keen observer. I think she really gets people and knows how we tick.

"What I want to know is . . . with all my education, all the classes I've attended or taught, and all those sermons—I guess I just want to know if I'm right about all of this."

And God said, "No. You are not completely and fully right. Neither is anyone else; nor have they ever been. Through the centuries, people have been too tightly focused on what they know, and in trying to define Me, they try to reduce Me to what they can understand. The primary message of Jesus is proclaiming the Good News of My Love to all people always, not to replace one legalism with another. The message of Love cannot be reduced to what you understand; it has never been and should never be about being theologically correct."

God spoke to Grayson Tucker, who said, "Yeah, I could be Your Adversary—I mean, I got nothin' to stay here for, Y'know?

"Well, I guess my qualifications for the job are that I'm quick on my feet, and that I'm a . . . scrapper.

"If you don't pick me, I guess the next best guy for the job is Vinnie. He's about halfway to Hell already, You know what I mean?

"My question is . . . why did you make me . . . y'know, a homosexual?"

And God said, "Every person is different, and each of you is made in My image to be who you are and how you are. When you live in shame, when you seek to hide who you are, how I made you, you distort My image to the world. Your sexuality is part of you and part of what makes you uniquely yourself, but there is much more to you than that. You are a child of God: your purpose in this life is to love and to allow yourself to be loved, not because you are gay or straight but because you are yourself. Be as you are."

God spoke to Early Miller, who said, "I don't know if I would *like* to serve as Your Adversary, Lord, but I would be willing to if that's what You want me to do. It is an interesting possibility, though, I have to admit.

"I'd like to think that I see things clearly, and I like to try to imagine what it's like to be somebody else.

"You know who'd be a good Satan is Mrs. Ralph Ketchum. She's tough as nails and scary as hell, if You'll . . . ah, excuse my French there.

"My question, Lord, is . . . I want to know why Judas Iscariot betrayed Your Son. That's always bothered me. Was it for the money? Was it because he was mad or jealous? Was it Your will for him to do that, or did . . . did the Devil enter into him and make him do it? And did You forgive him?"

And God laughed and said, "That's rather more than one question, barrister. As you know, a person's intentions are very rarely pure. Judas was devoured by some of the temptations many people face: money, power, jealousy, envy. It is Satan's job to exaggerate all of these, but it was Judas's choice. It was a terrible decision that Judas made, but even in that instance, I allowed his choice to stand. And even in that instance, there can be nothing done from which I Am not able to bring something good. I forgive all who will accept forgiveness."

God spoke to Vinnie Carlisle, who said, "Yeah, I'd love to be Satan—I mean, how cool would that be?

"I don't mind seeing people getting hurt or suffering and stuff; I'm okay with all that.

"I don't think any of these clowns would be as good as me, but if you're not up to the challenge of working with me or something, I guess that Tucker punk might be okay. He could probably stir up some trouble for you, but not as good as me.

"What I want to know is, what's in it for me? Do I get paid and have, like, vacation time and all that?"

And God said, "The compensation is not material. Satan sees reality as it is and sees Me in all of Creation. The Adversary of God serves an important purpose by giving My children the freedom of choosing between what is right, good and loving, or wrong, destructive and selfish."

"That's all?"

"That is enough."

God spoke to Trudie Svoboda, who said, "No, sir, I would not like to be the Devil. I guess I would if You told me I had to, but . . . well, I'd really rather not.

"The only thing about me that I could say might be suited to the job is that I'm accustomed to causing pain, and I see the necessity of it. But I don't like it.

"I think . . . um . . . Narni would be good. I hate to say that because I don't really know her all that well, but I don't know most of these people, just her and Father Mac and Early, and I wouldn't want either of them to leave. Leave . . . me, I guess. And some of those other people would just be mean. I guess I wouldn't want a mean person being the Devil—that would be a lot of power for some of these guys.

"My question is whether Jesus is the only way to Heaven. You know: He said 'I am the way, and the truth, and the life. No one comes to the Father except through me'—and if that's right, what happens to all those other people who aren't Christians?"

And God said, "You have two brothers and a sister."

Trudie was surprised, but she said, "Yes, sir."

God continued, "And your mother and father love all of you, even though you are different."

"Yes, sir."

"Even though your brother Patrick got into some trouble when he was in college, and they had to take him to a rehabilitation center in Tupelo."

Trudie took a sharp breath and whispered, "Yes, sir."

"Now, Trudie: Which of the four of you do you think your mother and father love the most?"

She said, "I don't . . . they love us all the same."

"They love you all differently, because you are different people, but they love you all with the same love, because you are all their children. Now consider this: every person ever born is My child, and I love all My children forever. Jesus of Nazareth is the perfect revelation of My grace for the world, and he proclaimed My Love for all: Jews, Gentiles, Romans, lepers, tax collectors, prostitutes, and all who would listen. The purpose for becoming incarnate in Jesus Christ is to communicate My grace and Love as fully as humans can understand it and to invite people to accept it.

"My grace and Love are not limited in any way. I do not love the Christians more than I love the Jews, the Muslims, or the Buddhists, or people who adhere to any other religion, or those who have rejected any religion at all, any more than your parents love you more than your brothers or your sister. What happens to the people who aren't Christians is what happens to all humans: they die, and they either accept My Love in whatever way they have found it, or they choose to love themselves."

God spoke to Luke Pivens, who said, "Yes, sir, I will do that. I am familiar with the power of temptation and the price which must be paid.

"If you do not choose me, let me suggest Vinnie Carlisle, especially if you're looking for someone with a penchant for cruelty.

"My question is . . . what about those who have never been loved at all? How will they receive your love so they can come home?"

"There are none who have never been loved, because I have always loved them and I put My Love in them. Tragically, there are some who have never been loved by any human, not even by their own mother or father, though I put it into all of you to love and care for your children. The bond between children and parents is primary, and it is often your best understanding of My Love for you. It is much more difficult for someone who has never been loved to accept My Love, but I will offer it forever. And I tell you this: you will not be whole until you ask your daughter for forgiveness."

God spoke to Mickey Doyle, who said, "Lord, if you need one of us to serve as Your Adversary, I will do it.

"I don't know if I would be well suited, but I've seen some terrible things in my life, and I believe I am tough enough. I also think I understand why You need an Adversary—I've seen light and dark, good and evil, and the consequences of bad choices, and still I believe that we need to be free to make real choices.

"If You are looking to invite someone other than myself, I guess I'd recommend that lady, Mary Elizabeth. She seems tough as nails, but she's got a good loving heart.

"The question I'd like to ask is . . . is my Virginia there, will I see her if I come . . . up there?"

And God said, "She is, and she will be waiting for you, whether you become My Adversary or not."

God spoke to Walter Johnson, who said, "Jesus—I will do what you want me to do, but if I'm bein' honest, I'm hopin' you ain't gonna ask me to be the Devil.

"I don't know 'bout bein' suited to it, though. You know 'bout that more than me.

"I don't really know none of these people but Miss Mully and Miss Narni. That Vinnie boy, I sure wouldn't want him, though, that's for damn sure. Sorry. I guess Miss Mully would be best, though, of her and Miss Narni. Miss Narni, she 'bout the sweetest person I ever met, so I'm gonna say Miss Mully. I sure would miss her, though.

"I know You said You ain't keepin' score and all, but my mama always tol' me that I had to go to church or the Devil would get me. Well, I ain't been to church since I was in Korea, when Sarge made us go—I guess You already know I ain't never really liked it much. And I want to know if goin' to church is worth all that bein' yelled at all the time."

And God said, "The purpose of the Church is to experience and share My Love as the people receive it through Jesus, by the power of the Holy Spirit. If you can find a church like that, it will be well worth it. I Myself would not attend a church that yells at Me all the time about the threat of Hell and damnation, preaching dread and fear and shame, portraying Me as an angry, vengeful God. If the message is not about Love, it is not about Me. Find a congregation who loves Me, and you will find a community you can love and who will love you."

God spoke to Millie Ketchum, who said, "Oh, Lord—I am just completely overwhelmed by all of this . . . and by Your love. I have wasted so much of my life keeping people away; if I could . . . if I could make up for it somehow, I . . . yes, I would be glad to serve as Your Adversary, if I could help.

"I don't know why I might be well suited, but I suppose I have become accustomed to people . . . keeping their distance.

"I think that Mickey, the bank guard, would be a good Adversary for you. I just think he knows who he is, more than some of the rest of us.

"Lord, is it . . . what I want to know is, is it too late for me to love and to be loved?"

And God said, "No, dear, it is never too late. You have seen through your own disguise, and I Am glad. Now you can show your true self. If you love, you will be loved; if you forgive, you will be forgiven. Every morning before your feet touch the floor, every night before your eyes close, say this: 'Love is the point of it all.'"

God spoke to Jeremy Adams, who said, "No, Lord, I would not like to serve You in that way, but . . . I will if You need me to. I mean, I guess I don't really know how much say we have in this, really, but if it's all the same to You, I guess I'd rather not.

"If You need me to be Your Adversary, I guess my best talent would be that . . . I think I'm very loyal.

"No, I think Tucker would be better. He knows how to tempt a guy, for sure, and he's . . . it would be a good thing to get him out of the situation he's in.

"What I want to know is why there is so much suffering and pain in the world. I mean, if You're all God and everything, couldn't You stop all that?"

And God said, "I could. I could make everything just perfect for everyone, for all time, and My children would lose their freedom to choose whether they believe in Me, whether they love Me or not. If everything was perfect all the time, if gratitude was the only choice, your freedom would be an illusion; it is no choice to pick between that good or another good. Humanity is created to love Me because they are free to choose it, not because of the lack of suffering and pain, but in spite of it."

God spoke to Narni Pivens, who said, "I will serve as Your adversary if that is what You want me to do.

"If I were Satan, I guess my sense of right and wrong would be useful, although now that I say that out loud, I'm not sure how.

"I think Mr. Doyle would be good. I think he's been a little lost since his wife died, and I think he needs some sense of purpose.

"My question is about Heaven and Hell, I guess. No—here it is: Why is what You've said about Heaven and Hell today so different from what we've been taught in church?"

And God said, "Some who have influence in the Church have either failed to understand that I Am not like them, limited in compassion and patience as they are, or they have manipulated their message to benefit themselves. They have found great power in the false message that the grace of God is conditional or is restricted to the people who believe or behave as they tell them. My grace is not limited; I Am eternal Love, Love that creates all that is, Love that never gives up on any of My children, ever. Some church leaders think that would be bad for business."

God spoke to Mary Elizabeth Sims, who said "Yes, Lord. I will do whatever You want me to do.

"I don't know what good I'd do bein' Satan, but I 'spect if You can take a young man all burnt up on a blazin' ship and make him into what You needed, You could make somethin' out of me, too.

"I don't want none of these people to have to be the Devil. I'd just as soon not know who the Devil is. I guess either one of them gang-sters—Vinnie or that quiet one who sat on the other side of Ben—I guess most people are sayin' one of them. But I don't want neither one of them, 'cause I'm afraid they'd make too much trouble, and life is hard enough without all that. So, if I have to say somebody, I'll say that snooty old woman, Miss Millie.

"You already answered my main question, Lord, 'bout why was Tallulah born the way she was, and You're right—I don't understand much of it. I guess I'm like a mouse tryin' to understand a magnet. But maybe they ain't nothin' wrong with bein' a mouse."

And with great tenderness, God said, "Do you remember taking Tallulah to the dentist when she was twelve? She had a cavity, and it was hurting her. Do you remember?" Mary Elizabeth nodded. "You had to hold her down, hold her head still while Dr. Hall gave her a shot, drilled her tooth, and filled the cavity, and the whole time you were telling her that she had to stop fighting, that Dr. Hall had to do this, that you were sorry it hurt her. But she didn't understand. She couldn't understand, and you knew that, too."

"That drill 'bout scared her to death."

"That night you made a peach cobbler just for her, to try to make up for it."

"That was her favorite," Mary Elizabeth sobbed, "that peach cobbler."

"And when you put her in her bed, she held on to you until she fell asleep. Then you went out on your porch and cried for an hour."

"Because it hurt her."

"Because it hurt her, because you had to let it hurt her, and because you could not explain it in a way that she could understand."

"Yes, Lord—I remember."

"I cannot explain this to you so that you can understand. I know that it hurt you that Tallulah was born as she was. I had to let it hurt you because for Creation to be perfect there must be all levels of perfect and imperfect. But Tallulah Mae Sims was always perfect in My eyes, just as your love for your daughter made her perfect in yours. And it showed your true heart."

Chapter 39

A Peach Cobbler Made in Heaven

They all opened their eyes at the same time and looked at the others sitting around the tables, each of them wondering the same things: Which of them would become the next Adversary of God? Which of them suggested that I should be Satan?

God said, "Thank you all very much for your honesty and for your questions. Six of you were not suggested by any of the others; if I call your name, you need worry about it no longer."

"Jeremy Adams."

"Yes, Sir?"

"You will not be invited to be My Adversary." Jeremy exhaled a long, slow breath, releasing an anxiety he had not been willing to acknowledge until that moment. He said, "Thank You, Lord." He found Narni's hand and squeezed it, whispering to her "Whew."

"Luke Pivens." Luke nodded once, accepting the decision without showing any emotion. "Very well. May I go now?"

"You have not been held here against your will, Luke. Grayson Tucker's debt to you is paid in full; you will find six thousand dollars in a paper bag on the front seat of your car. That is what he owed you. So you have received what you came here for, and I trust that you will leave him alone. I will remind you of what I said about becoming whole again." Luke Pivens stood and left Fuddy's without looking back.

Narni did not watch him go. Jeremy leaned toward her and whispered, "Pivens?"

"Yeah—my dad. It's a long, ugly story."

"When you're ready to tell it, I'll be here to hear it."

She squeezed his hand back.

"Thomas McBride."

Mac's first impulse was to say, "Just call me Mac," but he caught himself and said, "Thank You, Lord."

"Trudie Svoboda."

A sob rocked Trudie, and she put her face between her hands. "Oh, thank God!" Then she took her hands away and said, "I mean . . . thank You, Lord. Thank You!"

"Early Miller."

Early said, "Thank You, Lord." He was relieved, but he was a little troubled by the fact that nobody had voted for him. He hadn't wanted to be Satan, but he'd wanted to be considered. All of that evaporated in an instant when Trudie leaned over and said, "Drinks are on me." Early said it again, feeling it more fully: "Thank You."

Jeremy had recovered himself enough now to recognize that God had called five names, leaving just one more. Surely He wouldn't ask Narni to be His next Adversary. Clearly it would be that creep Vinnie Carlisle. Or maybe it would be Tucker, although part of the reason Jeremy had suggested him had just walked out the door. Or could it be the old lady who was so demanding and rude, what's-her-name Ketchum? Or the grizzled bank guard who'd held a gun on him? Or one of the homeless people, Walter or Miss Mully—oh, surely not Miss Mully. No, it's gotta be . . .

"Walter Johnson." All the humans took a sharp breath together and looked around the tables, calculating, speculating. With six eliminated, there were six remaining: Mickey, Tucker, Millie, Mary Elizabeth, Vinnie, and Narni.

Walter said, "Thank You, Sir. Please don't take Miss Mully away from me."

With infinite patience, the Lord God said, "Thank you, Walter."

Jeremy said, "And please don't take Narni!"

God answered, "Thank you, Jeremy."

There was no one to plead for the other four.

God continued, "As you have cut the number in half, I will halve it again. Grayson Tucker, Millie Ketchum, and Danny Royce Elkins will not be considered further."

There were all sorts of reactions to this, but none so quick or as loud as Vinnie's. He stood up, knocking his chair back so it clattered on the floor behind him, and shouted, "What the hell's wrong with you, you old fool? You think these idiots"—pointing toward Mickey, Mary Elizabeth, and Narni—"would do better than me? You're crazy as hell!"

"No, I Am not crazy," God said with His eyes twinkling, "but indeed Hell is. Nevertheless, it is My choice to make and not yours. You have other decisions you must make, which will determine the rest of your life."

"Go to Hell!"

"Yes, thank you, Danny Royce. I will. I hope that you will not."

Vinnie Carlisle kicked the chair out of his way and left with curses under his breath. Nobody watched him leave, either.

"Now I will have another conversation with these three."

Jeremy felt panic rising, threatening to take him over. "Lord, please!"

"Trust Me," was all God said.

God spoke to Mickey, Mary Elizabeth, and Narni, all three of them together. "I want each of you to know why I have chosen you.

"Narni, you would be a good Adversary because you are fair and compassionate. You pay attention to people and understand how their minds work.

"Mickey, you would be a good Adversary because you are durable and strong. You have seen some of the worst humanity has to offer, and you continue to offer yourself to maintain peace and order.

"Mary Elizabeth, you would be a good Adversary because you understand the pain of an imperfect world. You have been able to forget yourself in the service of another.

"One of you three will soon become My next Adversary, if you choose it. You understand that you will no longer be yourself but will be Satan, the Prince of Lies, until the moment comes that you renounce the role, at which time you will return to your human body. Then you will come to the decision all humans must make: to love Me or to love themselves more. Now, My children, think carefully what you want say to Me."

There was a long silence, and Mickey said, "Let Thy will be done, Lord. I will serve."

Narni said, "So will I. But . . . Lord, I will be Satan if that's what You want me to do, but . . . if it's okay with You, I'd rather not."

Mary Elizabeth said, "I will serve, if You need me. But I 'magine You already know I don't really want to."

God spoke to Mary Elizabeth. "Be at peace, dear one. You will soon be reunited with your daughter. She tells Me that she will serve you a peach cobbler made in heaven when you come Home to her at last."

God spoke to Narni. "Be at peace, Sweet Heart. You have your life to live, love to offer, and forgiveness to consider. Chase your dreams, and do not stop until you hold them in your hands."

God spoke to Mickey. "Michael, I invite you to become the next Adversary of God. Please understand that I will always love you, even when it seems you are working against Me. Will you consent to serve Me as Satan?"

"Yes, Lord. I consent."

Narni and Mary Elizabeth came to Mickey then, and the three of them gathered in a hug, all of them tearful for their own reasons. When they broke their huddle, Mickey Doyle said, "When should I . . . start?"

God said, "Perhaps the order of the universe will not become unbalanced if there is no Satan for a few days. You will have some time to visit Virginia's grave on the anniversary of her death and to find your dog a loving home."

Narni asked, "What kind of dog? What's its name?"

"Barney. He's just a mutt, but Virginia loved him. He's mostly Labrador retriever, but smaller, with a patch of white on his chest. She found him in the Walmart parking lot, starving and eaten up with fleas and mange, but she loved him and fed him and took him to the vet, and in a couple of weeks he was just part of the family. He's a good boy."

Narni said, "I'd be glad to take him, Mickey. I'll take good care of him, I promise."

Mickey was unable to speak, but he nodded.

God said, "Perhaps you could give him to Narni as a Christmas present. I suggest you bring Barney to the Christmas Eve service at St. Paul's on Sunday night."

Mary Elizabeth asked, "Will you be there, Lord?"

"I Am always there."

Chapter 40

What Do I Do Now?

Once again, they all opened their eyes at the same time, and God spoke to the ten people around the tables. "Mickey Doyle has agreed to serve Me as My Adversary."

There were congratulations offered and gratitude expressed for who was chosen and for who was not. When it calmed a bit, God said, "Narni, you will find a nice bottle of wine and a loaf of good bread in the refrigerator. Could you bring it out for us to celebrate?"

Narni knew without doubt that there had never been any wine or bread in the fridge at Fuddy's. She also knew she would find it there when she opened the refrigerator door. Jeremy stood up and said, "I'll help."

When they were both in the kitchen, Jeremy said, "Narni, I'm so sorry. I didn't mean what I said. I was just mad and hurt and stupid."

"Hush, Jeremy. It's okay."

"No, it's not okay. I love you, Narni. Please forgive me. I love you and I will go wherever you go. I don't want to step on your dreams. We can go to New York and you can break into the comics business, and I can . . . I don't know what I can do, but I'd love to go with you and we . . . we'll figure it out."

"Okay, we can talk about that later. But we have a dog now."

"A . . . dog?"

"Barney. We're taking Mr. Doyle's dog."

"We?"

"Yes—we."

Narni brought the bread and wine, and Jeremy found eleven coffee cups or glasses for the wine. Narni filled everyone's cup or glass without seeming to lessen how much was in the bottle. God took the bread and broke it, passing half of it to His right and the other to His left; everybody took as much as they wanted, and it seemed to Narni that they had more bread left over than they'd started with.

She looked at God questioningly, and He winked at her. Then He held up His glass and repeated His toast: "To Life, and to Love!"

Everyone held up their wine and repeated the toast with gusto. Then Early said, "Lord, may I ask a question?"

God laughed and said, "Another question. Yes, Early, ask it."

"Will we remember this? I mean, are You going to make us forget it?"

"You will remember what you choose to remember. However, you may find it difficult to speak of the events of this day with people who are not here with us in this moment. I suggest that the nine of you form a community, to remember."

Narni said, "That's a great idea! We can call ourselves the God Squad, or the Great Pie Society, or the Siblings of Satan."

None of those names seemed to take, and several expressed concern about the last one. God said, "I Am not so removed as you may have been taught. There have been other such fellowships, following other visits I have made. Some have kept it quiet; others have been denounced as heretics or witches, or labeled insane."

They all paused together to take that in, until Trudie suggested they could be Fuddy's Secret Fellowship, and everybody seemed to be fine with that. Then Narni said, "Mary Elizabeth, Mr. Doyle and I have already agreed that we're going to meet at St. Paul's for the Christmas Eve Midnight Mass. Can the rest of you join us?"

They all said they could, and Mac was delighted. Then Narni asked the priest, "Do you think the people will mind if Mr. Doyle brings me and Jeremy a Christmas present to the service? It's a dog."

Mac wasn't at all sure that the people of St. Paul's would be happy to have a dog in church, but Millie Ketchum didn't hesitate. "They will all be glad to welcome Mr. Doyle's dog, and all the rest of you—I will make sure of it."

God said, "Now the time has come for Me to leave you to live your lives."

The people around the tables groaned, and tears formed in many of their eyes. But God said, "Be of good cheer. You will see Me again, if you choose it. Until then, love one another, and love who you are. Look for what is True, let go of fear and shame, and accept the fact that I love you, each of you, all of you, and all of My children, forever."

Then He blew His breath on them until it became an unimaginably sweet wind, blowing so hard they all closed their eyes. When they opened them, they no longer saw Him.

Sunday was Christmas Eve, and St. Paul's was expecting a big crowd for the midnight service. Mac found the "Reserved for Family" signs they used for funerals and blocked off the first two pews on the left side, right in front of the pulpit. Millie Ketchum ushered each of the other members of the Fellowship to the front of the church. She almost had to pull Mr. Doyle up there, as he held poor squirming Barney, who'd never seen so many people in one place before. Mary Elizabeth said she and Walter couldn't possibly go to the front of the church, but Millie said they were her guests, and this was where they were supposed to be.

The congregation stood when the processional hymn started: "O come, all ye faithful," with diapasons booming. Nine of the Fellowship craned their necks to see the tenth, the Rev. Mac McBride, at the end of the procession.

Mac preached a short, powerful sermon. He asked the congregation to imagine what it must have been like for those shepherds "keeping watch over their flocks by night," when the angel of the Lord came to them. "They were just minding their business," Mac said, "just watching the sheep, and then all of a sudden, with no warning, there was an angel right there with them. 'And the glory of the Lord shone around them, and they were terrified.' Well, of course they were! We would be, too, right? I mean, what if you saw the angel of the Lord, what if you witnessed the birth of the baby Jesus, what if you saw God with your own eyes? You'd be scared to death if you walked into Fuddy's and God was sitting there having a piece of pie, wouldn't you?"

The congregation laughed demurely and murmured that they would be scared, and Mac continued. "But here's the thing. The angel told them Jesus was born and laid in a manger, a feeding trough for the livestock. It wasn't theological or mystical or especially divine—it was human, it was common, it was real. And it really happened.

"Jesus really was born in Bethlehem. And God is really with us still—with us this evening, with us tomorrow when we open our presents and eat too much Christmas dinner, with us the next day and the next day and the next. With us next time we go to the post office or the grocery story or Fuddy's.

"I think that's the reason we celebrate Christmas and the reason God became incarnate: to let us know that God is real and that God really loves us, all of us, all the time."

When they went up to receive the Eucharist, with Millie almost pulling Tucker to the altar rail—"Yes, you too!" Walter whispered to Mary Elizabeth, "This is just like when we had wine and bread at Fuddy's!" and Mac started laughing so hard he had to put his hand over the wafers so they wouldn't fall.

After the service, the members of the Fellowship waited for everyone to file out of the church, most of the people telling Mac what a wonderful sermon it had been and wishing him a Merry Christmas. Then the ten members of the Fellowship gathered in a tight circle in the vestibule, with a dog in the middle.

Mac said, "Thank you all for coming. I hope it was okay." Everybody said it was, and Walter asked if he could come back. Mac assured him that he and Mary Elizabeth and any of the rest of them would be more than welcome.

Millie added, "You let me know if anybody treats you poorly."

Tucker was struggling. He knew he should be relieved that he didn't have to pay his debt to Vinnie Carlisle, but he was starting to think he didn't know who he was anymore. Everything in his life was turned inside out. Jeremy saw his distress and said, "Tucker? You okay?"

"Oh, sure—I'm always . . . no. No, I'm not. I mean, I just saw God and Satan; what do I do now?"

They stood in awkward silence until Early Miller, lackadaisical lawyer and budding heretic nodded to himself, as if he'd made a decision. "Hey look, kid. Me and Mickey and Father Mac talked Lieutenant Durning into letting the bank robbery charges drop, since you didn't actually steal anything and the only person hurt was you. I'm about to change my practice, get out of wills and contracts and get into something more fun, something more meaningful. I'm thinking we've got people in this town who need some legal aid, maybe do a little public defender work, and I'm thinking I'm going to need some help. I don't know how much I'll be able to pay at first, but I've got a room over my office that you could stay in, and … maybe we could get you into college or see what happens. Whattaya say?" Early held out his hand to Tucker, who hesitated for the briefest of moments before taking it gratefully. Early said, "The first time I have any reason to think you're smoking dope or doing anything stupid, you're out, understand?" Tucker said, "Yes, sir."

"Well," Mac said, "while we're thinking how we can all help each other, this congregation builds a house every spring with a family who agree to work with us on it. Mary Elizabeth, if you and Walter were … ah … married, I think Millie and I could work it out so you could be that family and help us build you a home."

Mary Elizabeth and Walter looked at each other as if for the first time. Then Mary Elizabeth said, "We gonna need to talk about that, right, Dub?"

Dub said, "Yes, ma'am," which Mickey observed was a good start to any marriage.

It was Jeremy Adams who suggested that they make a "pinkie pledge" to come back the next Christmas Eve, and it was Narni Pivens who added that they should return every Christmas Eve, no matter where they lived. They all made a solemn pledge, each of them entwining their right little fingers in a knot in the middle—all of them but Mickey Doyle.

"Oh, Mickey," moaned Narni. "I'm so sorry, I . . ."

"I will be here," he said, "every Christmas Eve. You won't see me, but I'll be here. And if you ever feel like skipping it or griping that the sermon is too long or that you hate to get all dressed up, or you recognize that the church is full of hypocritical sinners, I hope you will remember that I'll be *especially* here in those moments."

Then the future Adversary of God knelt down and kissed his dog, scratching him behind the ears. "You're a good boy, Barney. Be sweet to Narni and Jeremy for your mother and me, okay?" Mickey went around the circle, hugging each one of them, until he got to Jeremy. "*Twenty-seven* green peanut M&M's?"

What Jeremy said was "Yes, sir," but what he thought was he'd missed one, and it didn't rain after all. Maybe things were looking up.

Jeremy and Narni walked slowly to her car, neither of them willing for the evening to end, both of them excited about the future. Barney had whined when Mickey walked away, but now he was more interested in smelling the messages the neighborhood dogs might have left on the trees and signposts they were passing. Narni had just put her head on Jeremy's chest, laughing at some silly thing he'd said, when he stopped and stood straight.

"What?" she said. "What is it?"

"Look," he said, nodding toward her car.

Luke Pivens was waiting for her.

Chapter 41

You the One Gettin' All Chewed Up

Soft and loving Narni was gone in a second, replaced by a woman filled with white-hot anger and deep hurt. Jeremy's first impulse was to run over and hit the guy in the mouth before he could say a word, but Narni clutched his arm tightly and whispered, "He might have a gun. Please don't do anything stupid."

Then, she said to her father, "I didn't think I would have to see you again."

"Yeah, well. Look, couple days ago the old guy said something I can't shake . . ."

"Just one thing?" asked Jeremy.

"You can just stay the hell out of this, pal."

"Or what?"

"Or I will break several of your bones."

Mickey Doyle was standing behind a tree, waiting to see if he was going to be needed. He had planned to watch until Barney got in the car, just to be sure, but now he wanted to see how this would play out. Jeremy wouldn't last five seconds if it came to a fight. He heard a snap to his right and saw Early Miller walking slowly toward Narni's car. He must have walked Trudie to her car on the other side of the park and was now about to blunder into this confrontation between Luke and Jeremy. Mickey held out his hand to tell Early to stop, put a finger to his lips, and then pointed at Jeremy, Narni, and Luke.

Early nodded. He liked Jeremy; he seemed like a sweet kid. Mostly clueless, a little slow on the uptake, but sweet. He wouldn't have a chance against a guy like Luke Pivens. He was glad Mickey was here. The two of them would make sure things didn't get out of hand.

Jeremy knew that Narni and her father both thought he would back down, and normally it would have been a safe bet. But he'd been thinking a lot about who he was and what he wanted to do with his life. And in this moment, Jeremy Adams decided he did not want to be pushed around anymore.

He walked over to Narni's father and said, "I am not afraid of you. If you've got something to say to Narni, say it and go away."

They stood looking at each other nose to nose, their breath frosting in the winter night. Then Luke said, "All right, kid—you got guts, I'll give you that. Let me just talk to my daughter for a minute, then I'll be gone."

Jeremy looked back at Narni, who nodded, and he stepped aside. She said, "Okay, I'm listening."

Luke looked around nervously, clearly uncomfortable. Narni glared back. "Look, uh . . . the old guy said if I didn't apologize to you, I would never be whole. I don't know who that guy was, but I saw some stuff I can't explain, so . . . y'know, maybe he's right. That's what I came to say: I'm sorry, okay?"

Narni stood impassively, waiting, but Luke was finished. "That's it? You murdered my mother, and I haven't seen you or heard from you for twenty years, and all you've got to say is tht you're sorry because you think it will help you? That's all you got?"

"Well, y'know—me and your mother had a tough marriage, and then we started doing heroin pretty hard. It was just another fight, really, that kind of got out of hand."

"Yeah," she said, with acid in her voice. "I guess it *kind of* got out of hand."

"I didn't know what I was doing!"

"You knew you were shooting heroin into your veins with a six-year-old in the house!"

"I wish I'd never done that. Any of it. And now I'm telling you, I'm trying to apologize."

"Okay, you've apologized. Now go away."

Luke Pivens stared at the young woman in front of him, so much like her mother it scared him. Then he turned and walked away.

Narni looked at Jeremy, who opened his arms for her to walk into. She cried for several minutes. Mickey gave Early a thumbs-up, and they both slipped away unnoticed. Jeremy held Narni tightly, with the dog Barney at their feet. "Oh, Jeremy—I know I'm supposed to forgive him. That's what God said. That's what Ben said, too, right before he . . . left. I ought to forgive him, but I just can't."

Jeremy held her even tighter and said, "I thought he meant you needed to forgive *me*." Then he said, "Look, we all know we need to forgive each other, right? But sometimes it might have to wait a while. You have to wait 'til you're ready. You can't just say you forgive something like that until you mean it."

Narni nodded. Then she heard Mary Elizabeth's voice in her head: "Hold on now, Sweet Pea. It ain't hurtin' your daddy one bit, you hatin' him like this. You the one gettin' all chewed up, an' it ain't hurtin' him at all."

Then there was another voice, rich and full, ringing like a carillon: "Hatred does not have to win forever." Her memory was flooded by that same beloved voice also saying, "Only love and faith can ever truly mend your heart."

"Damn it!" she muttered.

"What? Did I say something wrong?"

"No, just—get him back."

"Who?"

"My father. Get him back here."

"You sure?"

"Yeah. I might not ever get another chance. Get him back for me, would you?"

Jeremy ran off into the night and in a few minutes returned with Luke Pivens in tow.

Luke started, "Narni, I . . ."

She held up her hand. "Don't say anything, or I might not be able to do this." Luke nodded and stood quietly.

"I don't want to live in hate anymore. I don't want you to have that much power over me, to keep hurting me over and over, ever again. I want you out of my life, and out of my head. So . . . I forgive you. And I release you."

Luke started again, "Narni, I . . . ," and Jeremy looked at her and saw her shaking her head. He said to Luke, "That's it. Time for you to go your way."

Luke stood for a while, and then he turned and walked away a second time. Jeremy came to Narni and held her again.

She looked up at him, appreciating him more than she ever had before. "Thanks for coming to my rescue."

"You didn't need rescuing. I just couldn't stand there and do nothing. He's a creep. I'm sorry—I know he's your dad and all, but . . ."

"He's a creep. Yeah, I know. Are you cold?"

"Yeah—it's freezing out here!"

"How about if you come over and help me get Barney settled into his new home? I've got some eggnog and a little bit of something to put in it, and maybe we can . . . warm each other up a little bit."

Jeremy was not at all slow on this particular uptake.

Four Christmas Eves Later

"I'm free!" Mickey told the old lady proudly.

"You're *almost* three," his mother said. They were in the vestibule at St. Paul's before the Christmas Eve service, and Millie Ketchum was helping get the boy out of his snow coat, almost as large as he was.

"Where's Jeremy?" Millie asked.

"Parking the car," said Narni. "He let us out in front so we wouldn't get as wet."

"How's Barney?"

"He's great. He protects his puppy," she said, motioning toward Mickey, "but I think he's glad to get a break every once in a while."

Millie picked up the squirmy little boy and tried to hug him before she had to put him back down. "Mickey Doyle Adams, look how big you're getting!"

He said something that might have been "I'm free," but it was lost as he hid his face in his mother's skirt. Millie beamed and asked, "And how's the writing going?"

"Ah, well . . . it comes and goes. It's hard with two boys in the house."

"Two boys?"

"Well, Mickey and Jeremy. And it's just such an unbelievable story, I'm thinking maybe it would be more believable as a fiction."

Millie said, "A theological fiction?"

"Yeah, well—we'll see. How are you doing? I haven't seen you out and about much."

"I've been traveling. I went to Asheville to see my son and his wife and their extremely active little girls—five and seven, and acting like teenagers already! Then Gene and I went on an Alaskan cruise up to Ketchikan and stayed there for . . ."

"Gene? Who's Gene?"

"Oh, he's . . . a man about my age. I met him on an online dating site for mature singles. He lives in Chattanooga, but he's here tonight; I wanted him to meet the Fellowship."

"Have you told him about that afternoon at Fuddy's?"

"No, of course not! Who would believe it?"

Jeremy came up and joined them. "Hey, Miz K!" he said, kissing her on the cheek.

Narni teased, "Millie is . . . seeing someone."

"Mazel tov!" They looked at him blankly, and he said, "What? I've played a couple of bar mitzvahs in the last few weeks—it means congratulations, and good luck."

"So you're staying busy, doing well?" Millie asked.

"Yes, ma'am. I'm booked pretty solid. I'm not playing any major venues yet, but I've got a lot of small engagements, and I've got some time for writing my own stuff."

"He's sent a demo to an agent, who told him—"

"Well, hold on now," interrupted Jeremy. "Let's don't count that chicken before it's even an egg, okay?"

Narni put her arm around his waist and said, "We're chasing our dreams. Thank you, Millie."

That reminded Jeremy of something important, and turning to Millie, he said, "Thank you for all your help, Miz K. I've got a check for you." He started fumbling for his wallet.

Millie said, "I've told you, that was a gift. What's the point of having money if you can't spend it on people you love?"

"No," said Jeremy. "It's important to me to pay you back. I could never have afforded such a nice guitar without your help, and it's made a huge difference. I am going to pay you back."

"Just take care of your family, Jeremy—that's all the payment I'll ever need. You can pay me back later if you really have to."

They were still discussing the issue when Mr. and Mrs. Walter Johnson came into the vestibule. He was wearing a suit, and she was wearing a dark blue dress and new white tennis shoes.

Jeremy hugged Walter and exclaimed, "Woohoo—look at you, all dressed up!"

"Yeah," said Walter. "Ain't we pretty?"

Millie said, "Mary Elizabeth, you look lovely."

Mary Elizabeth made a nice curtsey and turned around so they could admire her dress. "Walter bought me a sewing machine. I made this dress myself."

Narni said, "I like your shoes, too."

"Well," said Mary Elizabeth somewhat sheepishly, "my friend Millie gave me a whole bunch of new shoes, and all of 'em in my size, too. Some of 'em would probably look better with this dress. But they mostly made me stand up too tall, felt like I was always 'bout to fall over. I like these right here, though. And my feet don't get cold."

Millie nodded and said, "No, I think that's fine. You and I are coming to the age of sensible shoes now. I might start wearing sneakers, too." Then she leaned over and whispered to Mary Elizabeth, "We can take those other shoes back. I kept the receipts."

Mary Elizabeth whispered in reply, "I don't know why somebody'd want a whole closet full of shoes anyway."

Millie Ketchum was spared from either having to agree with her or to admit she still had a closet full when Early Miller came in, with Trudie Svoboda on his arm, and Grayson Tucker a few steps behind. Early said, "It's starting snow out there."

After the service, when the congregation had all left, and after Millie's Gene had been introduced around and excused himself to go to his hotel before the roads got too bad, the Fellowship gathered in the parish hall, just as they had every year since their first Christmas Eve service after that afternoon at Fuddy's. There were no gifts exchanged and no need for any; the Fellowship itself was the gift.

They chatted for a while, each of them taking their turn at holding little Mickey until he'd had enough. He had slept through the service, which was all you could hope for in an almost-three-year-old, but now he was wide awake and getting cranky.

Narni stood up. "Y'all, I hate to have to do this, but I've got to get this little one home and in bed. Santa Claus is coming tonight!"

Mac was just coming in from the parish kitchen with a tray of wine glasses and a bottle of champagne. "Yes, but first we have to have the toasts!" When Narni seemed like she was about to resist, he said, "It's our tradition" quite firmly, and she sat back down.

A few years earlier, Mickey Doyle had lost his bank guard cap in the alley behind Star Comics; now, every year they used it as the hat for drawing out two names, the people who would offer the toasts. Mac solemnly picked out a small piece of paper and said, "Walter Johnson."

Walter stood up and raised his glass. "To life, and to love!" The other eight members of Fuddy's Secret Fellowship repeated the toast, and Walter picked the other name, announcing, "Grayson Tucker."

Tucker stood straight and tall and looked around the room at his friends. He had come into himself in the last few years and was doing well in his first year of law school. He lifted his wine glass and made the second toast: "To Mickey Doyle!" They all said, "Mickey Doyle!" and the little boy, amazed that they all said his name at the same time, said, "I'm free!"

Narni leaned over and picked up her son. "Yeah—we all are." As she looked around, she saw that they were all in complete agreement. "And that's a good thing, to be free."